Mostly Sunny

with a chance of storms

marion roberts

ALLEN&UNWIN

To Susannah Chambers – best and trusty editor,
despite being an avid objector to the word *iota*.

First published in 2009
Copyright © Marion Roberts

Allen & Unwin
83 Alexander St
Crows Nest NSW 2065
Australia
Phone: (61 2) 8425 0100
Fax: (61 2) 9906 2218
Email: info@allenandunwin.com
Web: www.allenandunwin.com

National Library of Australia
Cataloguing-in-Publication entry:
Roberts, Marion, 1966-
Mostly sunny with a chance of storms
978 1 74175 859 7
A823.4

Cover and text design by Design by Committee
Cover illustration by Ali Durham
Printed in Australia by McPherson's Printing Group

3 5 7 9 10 8 6 4 2

1.

I **was fresh** back at Mum's place after spending the weekend with Dad and Steph and my new baby half-sister, Flora. True to form, Mum had me doing chores within the first five minutes. I'd hardly even said hello to Willow before I found myself bundling the washing off the line because it looked as if it was about to bucket down.

Would you believe Mum chose the moment right when I had my arms full of half-dry socks and undies, to tell me the biggest piece of news since I found out Flora had been born.

'Sunny,' Mum said, bunching a sheet into the laundry basket. 'I've got some exciting news. At least, I hope you'll think it's exciting.'

'You're not having a baby are you, Mum? Because lately

that's what people have meant when they've said they have exciting news.'

Mum laughed and looked a little embarrassed. 'Ah, no, sweetheart.'

'Disneyland?'

'Not quite.'

'What then?'

Mum unpegged the last of the washing, and I heaped my pile onto the top of the basket.

'Well, you know how you just loved your grandmother's big old house?'

'Yep.'

'How would you feel about moving there? All of us. Granny Carmelene's house is ours now. She left it to me in her will.'

Mum looked dead excited, and I guess she thought that I'd be excited too. And maybe I should have been. I mean, it's not every day your family finds out they've inherited their very own big old white-and-black mansion. But to be honest, I found the idea about as exciting as a wet sock, and I guess it showed on my face.

'I thought you'd be thrilled, Sunny,' said Mum. 'You love that old house.'

'I *loved* the house because it was Granny Carmelene's. When she was *alive*! I can't imagine living there *now*. It'd be sad.'

2

'There's always the option to sell it, Sunny, but—'

'That'd be even *sadder*! What if dodgy developers bought it and turned it into fifty apartments? Granny Carmelene would—'

Just then, Willow came hurtling out the back door and raced at full greyhound-speed around the side of the house to the front gate. She must have heard it clicking open with her supersonic hearing.

'Aaaagh!' came Saskia's voice. 'No jumping, Willow! Down! *S-u-u-u-n-n-y!*'

'I think she might need rescuing,' said Mum, picking up the laundry basket. 'I'll take this lot inside. We'll talk more later.'

'Willow!' I called. '*Come, Willow!*' Within moments she was circling me frantically, doing laughing-hyena laps of the clothesline, looking over her shoulder the whole time, hoping I would chase her. I stood up tall and clicked my fingers.

'Willow, *sit*!' I said in my best obedience-school voice. But she must have heard the gate clink open again because instead of sitting she streaked back to the front of the house. It was Lyall coming home, and by the sound of his voice he was finding Willow's welcoming ceremony a little less distressing than Saskia had.

'That dog needs help,' said Saskia, wiping the side of her face with her scarf. 'She tried to bite my earlobe.'

Willow finally came trotting back, puffing like anything. with a look on her face that said, *Oh, sorry, Sunny, you asked me to sit, didn't you? I knew I'd forgotten something.*

I made the 'sit' hand signal again (because apparently they work better on dogs than words do), and Willow sat up tall at my feet and said, *I'm a good girl, really, Sunny, most of the time.* Just to be sure, I held her by the collar.

'Hey, Sunny, you're back,' said Lyall, dumping his bag. 'Did you hear the news?'

'*Shoosh, Lyall,*' urged Saskia through clenched teeth. 'Dad said not to say anything yet.'

'News about what?' I asked.

'About how we're going to be moving into your Grandmother's old place.'

'Lyall-luh!' squealed Saskia, punching his arm. He shrugged her off as if she were a blowfly.

''Course I know,' I said casually. 'What do you think I am, Lyall, chopped liver?' I averted my gaze downwards and noticed my knuckles all clutching and white, strangling the life out of Willow's collar. 'Come on, Willow,' I said, making my way to the back door. I marched down the hall and stomped straight past Mum in the kitchen. Then I slammed my bedroom door as hard as I could, hoping I might even shatter a window or two, because that would really be saying something along the lines of, *Good one, Mum. Make sure I'm the last to know, why don't you.* Can

4

you imagine? Even the precookeds knew before I did.

I sat on the bottom bunk feeling dead powerful for my door-slamming effort, and for how the whole world was locked on the other side.

Then I slouched on the bottom bunk and waited, because everyone knows when you slam the whole world out, you're secretly hoping that the world will barge back in and say, *Whatever is the matter, Sunny?*

But no one came, not even Willow. I felt pathetic, like Eeyore, and I soon realised that there were certain things (like Mum coming to rescue me in my sulkiest Eeyore moments), that had been left behind in the good old days before Carl and his kids moved in.

To make matters worse, I could hear the muffled voices of Mum and Lyall and Saskia from the kitchen, and I'm pretty sure they were laughing and saying cringeable things like, *Just leave her be,* and *Sunny just needs some Time Out.*

Finally, Willow wedged her snout sideways under the door, making small sooky whimpers.

'Come on, girl,' I said, opening the door just enough for her to squeeze through. I even let her jump up on the bed because there was nobody about to tell me not to, and we lay down together with both our heads on the one pillow, and I told her all the reasons why moving into Granny Carmelene's big old white-and-black mansion was the dumbest idea on earth.

For starters:

- ☀ My school is exactly three minutes away from here, my favourite and only home. I can make it on time even if I accidentally sleep in until five to nine (provided I skip breakfast and don't do my hair).

- ☀ If we move, my best friend, Claud, would suddenly be a long bus-ride away. What is the point of a best friend who lives on the other side of town?

- ☀ Claud and I happen to be co-owners and operators of Pizza-A-Go-Girl, a successful Friday night pizza delivery business that is right on the verge of going world-wide. Granny Carmelene's doesn't have a shed or a wood-fired pizza oven. Surely Pizza-A-Go-Girl would become Pizza-A-Gone-Girl in five minutes flat.

- ☀ There is no beach at Granny Carmelene's. There is a big chance Willow would sink into doggie depression if she can't race about on the sand. (The fact that the new house has its own private patch of river in no way makes up for this.)

- ☀ Boris would most definitely not survive another move, as it's a well-known fact that cats are bad at travelling.

- ☀ I am a person who isn't so good with change. And, let's face it, I've had to adjust to a lot lately: Carl and his kids moving in; my baby sister, Flora, being born;

Mum giving up smoking. I mean, another big change could really tip me over the edge.

☀ Living in a huge mansion might make us become big fat rich snobs.

☀ How about all those paintings at Granny Carmelene's with the accusatory eyes that follow you around the room and make you feel guilty for stuff you haven't even done? Seriously, who needs that?

☀ There would most definitely be a higher likelihood of tubes with fangs living at Granny Carmelene's. Everybody knows snakes live near rivers, and besides, Mum even told me that there are tiger snakes there, and they're not the type of snake to slither away when they hear you coming, they're the type of snake that chases you.

Willow agreed with every one of my points (except maybe the one about Boris), until Carl came home and she jumped down from my bed and scratched at the door to be let out. I closed the door quietly behind her, not feeling ready to go and join the others. My anger with Mum had given way to throat-aching sadness. The very thing I'd been trying to stomp and slam away.

You see, I hadn't told Willow that the real reason I was so upset was not because I didn't *want* to move into Granny Carmelene's house, it was simply that I couldn't *bear* to.

Since Granny Carmelene had passed away, I'd been doing my very best not to think about her. Not one little bit. Even the slightest memory made me giddy and sad and feel as if I had to sit my whole body down – like after a gut-wrenching rollercoaster when you have to put your head on your knees and wait for the world to stop spinning.

Every single inch of Granny Carmelene's house was soaked in memories and would make me ask questions that, as far as I knew, nobody could help me answer. Questions like: Where exactly does a person go when they stop being *somewhere* and you suddenly have to deal with them being *nowhere*. I mean, where exactly is *nowhere*?

2.

I figured the best approach was to simply ignore the whole *moving into Granny Carmelene's house* thing entirely. I stayed in my room until the last possible moment. Back in the good old days I would have been able to extend the last possible moment basically forever, but these days there was a real chance I would miss out on being fed. Especially with Lyall around. So I just slipped into my place at the table without saying anything at all.

We ate in perfect silence until Saskia had to go and spoil it. 'Come on, Sunny, the whole house is surrounded by oodles and poodles of lawn. Willow would love it.'

Mum and Carl both looked up hopefully from their dinner plates, and I gave them both *the eyebrow*.

Lyall shovelled his last wedge of roast potato into

his mouth then leant over with his fork and stole one of Saskia's.

'Lyall! Manners, please,' said Carl. Then he turned to me and said very earnestly, 'Sunny, I understand your reservations, but we *do* have to make a decision at some stage. Preferably soon.'

'It's true, Sunny,' said Mum. 'A house like that needs to be lived in. It's what your grandmother would have wanted.'

'Mum, are there any more potatoes?' I stood up, went into the kitchen and brought the baking tray back to the table. 'Who else wants some more?' I asked. 'There's probably enough for one more each.'

'Me please!' Lyall and Saskia sung out. Carl nodded too.

'When would we move then?' I asked, looking Mum straight in the eye.

Until Saskia blurted out, 'Next week!'

'Saskia!' Carl scolded.

And it was right at that moment that I realised moving to Granny Carmelene's was inevitable. I was totally outnumbered. Everyone was just going through the motions of having a discussion about it to make me feel as if I had some kind of *choice*. Mum had probably already booked the removalists. I tried to hold Mum's gaze but she was busy trying to catch Carl's eye for some support.

'More wine, love?' he asked, filling up her glass.

'Well, Mum?' I asked.

And because she knew she was completely busted she lowered her voice and said, 'We more or less tossed about the idea of being out of here just before the end of term. Then we'd have the whole winter holidays to settle in.'

Lyall and Saskia took to the task of eating their potatoes with similar levels of concentration required for a maths exam.

'So, what you really mean, Mum, is that we're moving *next week*, like Saskia said?'

'Really?' she said. 'Gosh, no, that can't be right? Is it that soon, Carl?'

'The end of next week,' confirmed Carl. 'And you get to take the Friday off school!'

'Terrific,' I said.

'And we're all getting new beds!' squeaked Saskia, earning herself a triple glare from Lyall, Mum and Carl.

'Can I please leave the table?' I asked, putting my knife and fork together.

'Sure, sweetheart,' said Mum.

'Can I have your potatoes?' Lyall asked with his mouth full.

'Knock yourself out, Lyall.'

I left my half-eaten meal on the table, went back to my room and climbed up to the top bunk – because I didn't feel like any company, not even from Willow. Plus, it's always in the top bunk that I come up with my best inventions. I was going to need something, fast! Some kind of state-of-the-art anti-grief contraption, kind of like my trusty old Stash-O-Matic, which used to hold all my secrets until I threw it into Bass Strait. A Sad Thoughts Obliterator? A No-Thinky-Granny-Thingy?

Mum came in eventually to tuck me in. She must have sensed I wasn't in a talking mood becuase she just kissed me on the forehead and gave me one of her *it's all going to be okay* looks.

I lay awake most of the night waiting for the perfect design to come. But nothing did. Not even eventually.

Then, right when I was about to give up, they arrived. Not a contraption, but a duo. Bruce and Terry. Grief bouncers. Who would have thought?

Bruce and Terry were just like those guys you see outside nightclubs whose job it is to keep the riffraff out. It was brilliant! With Bruce and Terry on the door, I could be assured that no nasty, throat-achy feelings would be allowed access to my brain. While Bruce was keeping sad feelings away, Terry would be preventing big questions from barging in. With *no* sad thoughts and *no* big questions, maybe I could be happy at Granny Carmelene's after all? I mean, stranger things have happened, right?

'Ahem, Miss, before we clock on as your personal

Grief Bouncers, we are required to ask for a *brief* – a set of instructions, if you will. Oh, and I'm Bruce. Pleased to be invented by you.' Bruce held out his hand and shook mine.

'Pleased to meet you too,' said Terry.

'I like your suit,' I said as he shook my hand. (Don't ask me why, but Bruce and Terry were definitely retro. I must have imagined them from one of those old cop shows. Bruce wore a tight shirt and flares, and Terry was in a chocolate-brown suit with the widest lapels ever.)

Realising that it wasn't polite to stare at other people's clothes for too long, I got out my notebook and scribbled down a list of instructions.

No sad thoughts
No achy throat
No missing of Granny Carmelene
No wondering where on Earth (or not on Earth) she might have gone
No grief of any kind.

Bruce read the list and then passed it to Terry.

'Not a problem, Sunday,' said Terry. 'You can take it from me that you will not have *one* sad thought about that grandmother of yours. Not one.' Terry wore a gold chain and spoke in a British accent a lot like how Carl sounds when he's pretending to be Michael Caine. He also pointed at me when he spoke, as though I was in trouble, which gave me a lot of confidence in his abilities.

'Even if I'm living in her house, Terry? Can you be absolutely sure?'

'Tell you what,' said Terry. 'You have *one* sad thought, and we'll give you your money back – guaranteed. Won't we, Bruce?'

Bruce nodded earnestly.

'I'll give it a go then,' I said, suddenly feeling very tired. For a moment, I pictured Granny Carmelene's big old house, as empty as can be, on its own bend in the river. And I remembered how it also had a tower (Granny Carmelene said it was called a *turret*), which had the cutest red carpety stairs leading up to it from the second storey landing. And I thought about how if we *did* move into the big old white-and-black mansion, the turret could possibly be my bedroom. Can you imagine? My own tower! (That's if the precookeds didn't suddenly want it for themselves. Siblings, I tell you; the minute they see you want something they become desperate for it themselves. They can't help it; it's in their breeding.)

3.

You'll be really pleased to know that I'm not going to tell you about the actual moving. Let's face it, even if we were rock-stars or royalty I'd be stretching it to find something interesting to say about packing our whole life up into boxes. Especially if you have a full-blown aversion to cardboard like I do.

Let's just say that moving had one major advantage. We got rid of Boris, the meanest brute of a cat that ever lived. Who would have thought? It was Carl's idea, because of him being an environmentalist, and all the wildlife Boris was sure to destroy the minute he was let loose at Granny Carmelene's. Don't get me wrong, it wasn't that Boris got *put down* or anything. He went to live with Lyall and Saskia's mum, so *technically* they still owned him. Perfect. I could tell Willow was also dead relieved when she watched Boris getting packed into his cat box and taken away in Carl's car.

It was a cold old winter morning, and even though I was meant to be helping with the moving, and even though I could only find one glove, I wanted to take Willow for one last run on Elwood beach. To say goodbye.

'Twenty minutes, Sunday!' Mum called as Willow and I disappeared out the front gate.

''Kay!' I hollered back. 'Come on, Willow, we'll have to run.'

On the way I said goodbye to absolutely everything. I said goodbye to every house in our street and every house on the way to the oval. I let Willow off her leash to do one last lap of the grass before clipping her back on as we made our way down to the canal. I said goodbye to the shopping trolley that Buster Conroy had pushed over the edge last summer. I said goodbye to every bridge along the way and to all the tiles with the stories on them. (Even though Claud and I wished we could have made the stories a whole lot better by including Street Poetry.) I said goodbye to Jerry's Milk Bar and Marine Parade, and as I crossed the road I looked up to Uncle Quinny's apartment block and said goodbye to that as well. I let Willow off her leash again and she did crazy circles around the grass near the beach.

I said goodbye to the monkey bars and the footbridge that Willow used to be too scared to cross, and I ran up the grassy hill right to the top of Point Ormond. There I stood up high on one of the concrete pylons and looked across the whole bay and the whole city, and Willow stood beside me, puffing and smiling.

'Bye-bye, Point Ormond,' I said, tagging the side of the tower and making a run for it down to the beach. Willow ran at full speed along the bluestone wall before flying off onto the sand in pursuit of a seagull. I said goodbye to the stale-hot-chip-smelling kiosk on the way.

Without knowing it was her last, Willow dug a frantic hole in the sand and stuck her snout deep down inside. Then, just as if she'd been bitten on the nose by a crab, she took off in full greyhound fashion down the beach. I was kind of worried she might be in the mood for finding something dead and revolting to roll in and knew Mum would be super unimpressed if we arrived home with Willow needing a bath.

'*W-i-l-l-o-w!*' I yelled after her, but the wind blew my voice straight back to me. Still, she must have heard a smidgen of it because she actually did run back, and then straight into the water to cool off.

When we got home, the entire house had been emptied and the guys in the removalist vans were strapping in all the pot plants, Willow's kennel and the stuff from the shed – like bicycles, my old scooter, my Totem Tennis pole and my pogo stick. I ran and said goodbye to the shed while no one was in there and then made my way back to the house.

'There you are, Sunny,' said Mum, putting her arm around me. 'You all set? My car is completely loaded up, so you go with Carl and the others and I'll follow, okay?'

'I've just got to say goodbye to my bedroom, Mum,' I said, suddenly feeling nervous that I might be left behind.

It didn't feel at all like the house I'd spent my whole life in. There were no traces of life left in it, just bare walls and clunky wooden floors echoing through the empty rooms that used to be my world. I looked about my old yellow bedroom. There was paint peeling off in all sorts of areas that were usually covered with furniture.

'Bye-bye, old bedroom,' I said, staring up at the bare light globe hanging from the ceiling. *Bruce and Terry better be on the job*, I thought to myself.

4.

As Carl pulled up in the driveway, my first impression was that Granny Carmelene's house looked dead spooky, especially as it was winter and some of the trees were bare, like bony fingers clawing up at the sky.

It was *really* hard not to think about the last time I'd seen the house (with an alive grandmother inside), but I didn't feel sad. I just felt… blank, and while feeling blank might not be very exciting, it sure is better than feeling tragic

'Nice one, Bruce and Terry,' I said to myself.

'What was that, Sunny?' said Carl.

'Windermere,' interrupted Lyall, reading the black lettering above the front verandah.

'Sunny's mum already told us about that, Lyall,' said

Saskia. 'It's the name of some old lake in England. I bags being the first one inside!' Saskia shot out the car door with Lyall right behind her, while I was kind of stuck because I had to hold Willow in case she ran away.

'Don't worry, Sunny,' said Carl, turning off the engine, taking the keys from the ignition and dangling them up near the rear-view mirror. 'They won't get far without these.'

'Maybe I should leave Willow in the car for a while,' I said. 'Just until Mum arrives and the vans are gone and we can lock the front gate.'

'Ah, no thank you, Sunny,' said Carl. 'Your mother told me how Willow chewed through all four seat belts in her car. And the handbrake!'

Willow looked a little embarrassed, as if to say, *Ease up, Carl, that was when I was a puppy, and they did leave me all alone in the car for a whole hour.*

'I'll just keep her on the leash then,' I said. 'Come on, Willow.' And I tried to get her to have a wee on the grass, because often it's the first thing she thinks of doing when she gets inside a new house.

Lyall and Saskia were peering through the front window into the library.

'Oh my goodness, Sunny!' said Saskia. 'Did your grandmother actually *read* all those books?'

'Now, you two,' said Carl in a stern voice. 'Let

Sunny show you around, and remember, if you can't agree nicely about bedrooms we'll be drawing them out of a hat.' He swung open the heavy front door, and Lyall and Saskia rushed in, just as Mum arrived with her car packed full.

I started to follow them in, but as I approached the big heavy door I couldn't help imagining Granny Carmelene being carried out of it on some sort of stretcher (or however it is that they carry people who have died in their sleep). And then I began to wonder things like: *Where do they take dead people to anyway?*

'Now, listen here, Miss,' said Terry, suddenly appearing in the doorway with his arms crossed. 'That sort of thinking is going to do you no good at all!'

'He's right,' said Bruce, shouldering past Terry. 'Now, listen up, Sunny. You've got important work to do. If you don't claim that turret room, those precooked siblings of yours are going to be all over it. You dig?'

Terry took something out of his jacket pocket. It looked like a tiny can of fly spray.

'What's that?' I asked, starting to feel a little urgent about getting inside to join the others.

'This, my friend,' said Terry, spraying a fine mist all over me, 'is what you might call *grief repellent*.' He showed me the label on the front of the can.

WOE-BE-GONE

Quick Knockdown

Kills Sorrow Fast

Multi Purpose Low-irritant Anti-grief Spray

'That should do it,' he said. 'Now you better get inside, Sunny!'

Bruce and Terry were right. I had to stop those precookeds from taking the bedroom that was rightfully mine. I took a deep breath and stepped inside.

'It's enormous!' Saskia was saying as she twirled around and around the tiled floor of the entrance hall. 'I can't believe we're actually going to live here!'

Lyall was heading for the library.

'Hey, hold up!' I said. 'I'm in charge of showing you around, remember?' I put on my best tour-guide voice. 'Ladies and Gentleman, as you can see, Windermere has been constructed from the finest materials money can buy. You will notice each tile in the entrance hall is made from the same marble as the Taj Mahal, and the walls are panelled with mahogany hand-cut from ancient forests by monks.'

'Oh, for sure, Sunny. That's not even funny,' said Saskia. 'You're just weird.'

'I'm sorry, Miss, there will be time for questions at the end of the tour.' I continued. 'Now, to our *raart* you will notice the *laaarbrary* and to our left the famous drawing

22

room. If you continue straight ahead you will find the master bedroom, the gameless games room, the dining room, the conservatory, the kitchen, the laundry and the study. Or you can take the stairs to the second floor where you will find three double bedrooms, all with ensuites, and of course Windermere's very own private observation tower fully equipped with its own super-duper telescope.

'Now, if you wouldn't mind coming this way I'd like you to experience the drawing room, which, you may remember from the guide book, is where Sunny Hathaway first sat and waited while Granny Carmelene made tea, on the occasion of their first meeting.'

'I'm with Saskia,' said Lyall. 'You're just plain weird, Sunny.'

'Please come inside quietly,' I said ushering them both into the drawing room. 'Have a seat.'

There were two grass-green velvet armchairs in front of a fireplace and Lyall and Saskia both ran to sit in the same one. Typical.

'No, Lyall!' screeched Saskia as he tried to push her onto the floor.

I sat quietly on the other chair, with Willow on a short leash sitting gently at my feet. 'They can see you, you know, and they think you're pathetic,' I said.

'Who?' asked Lyall.

'*Them*,' I said, nodding to the paintings crowded onto

every patch of wall: big ones, small ones, a huge one above the fireplace, and in every single one of them an eerie-looking old person with accusing eyes that followed you around the room. 'The *Scrrrrutin-eye-zers.*'

Lyall and Saskia stopped fighting one another and looked at the portraits more carefully

'Eeeew, creepy,' said Saskia 'They're looking right at me!'

'No, they're not. They're looking at *me*!' said Lyall. 'How do they do that?'

'They're actually looking at me too,' I said. 'That's what they do. That's why I call them the Scrrrrutin-eye-zers. Mwa ha ha ha!'

'Don't, Sunny!' squealed Saskia, turning her face to the back of the chair. 'Make them stop! Where's Dad?'

Lyall was pretending not to be freaked out, but the more portraits he noticed staring at him, the paler he became.

'You think that's scary, Lyall? Imagine how I felt when I was sitting here all alone being scrutinized by a whole roomful of portraits and then one of them actually *spoke*!'

Saskia looked as though she might burst into tears.

'It's a joke, silly!' said Lyall. 'Isn't it, Sunny?'

But I just gave Lyall *the eyebrow*.

Lyall leapt off his chair and made for the door, with Saskia right behind him, clutching the back of his top so she could keep her eyes shut while he led the way.

'Hey, you two! I've only just started the tour. Wait up.'

'Yeah, well, I'm kind of ready to have a tour of the garden!' said Lyall.

'Me too!' said Saskia.

I ran ahead of them to regain control as tour operator, and because I could tell Willow was keen to get outside, meaning that at any moment she might be prone to having *an accident*, which in her case means wee.

There was a huge old key in the back door, which I was finding difficult to unlock. Saskia was still snivelling and wiping her eyes, while Lyall kept flicking glances over his shoulder as if he were expecting to see one of the people in the portraits walking right down the hall after him.

'Hurry, Sunny,' he said. 'Open up.'

All four of us (Willow included) spilled out the door and onto the back verandah, then down the steps and onto the Botanical Gardensy spongy grass.

I pointed to the weeping willow by the river. 'There's a rickety old jetty down there and even a little river boat. Come and I'll show you.'

Willow tugged on her leash, wanting to be set free. 'Okay then, Willow, but stick by me, okay?' I unclipped her and she circled around all of us excitedly as we made our way down to the river. Her circles got bigger and bigger until something caught her eye and she shot out of sight.

That's when we heard the unmistakable screeching of

a cat, followed by a yelp from Willow and a loud thump, like something being knocked over. Then there was roaring from a really angry man, a second thud, a second yelp, and then Willow was scurrying back towards us with her tail between her legs. She buried her nose deep between my knees.

'What was that?' yelled Lyall.

'Could be anything,' I said putting Willow's leash back on. 'Let's go see.'

'How 'bout let's *not* go see?' whined Saskia, but Lyall and I were already running towards where we had heard the commotion. Saskia followed, so I guess in the end she didn't want to be left by herself.

On the other side of the orchard was a cottage surrounded by a faded picket fence. I suddenly remembered seeing it when Granny Carmelene and I had had our little tea party down under the willow tree.

'That's right!' I said. The gate to the cottage garden was wide open. 'There used to be some old man who lived here. The gardener, I think.'

Willow was hesitant, but Lyall and Saskia were already thumping about on the verandah and peering through the front window.

'Cool!' said Lyall. 'My own pad!

'It's not yours, Lyall! Anyway, I'm going to need an art studio,' said Saskia. 'It's perfect.'

That's when the front door of the cottage opened all by itself, and out of the shadows came the meanest looking old man you've ever seen in your life. On crutches. And, with a bandage across his hundred-year-old nose.

'You go away, you hear me?' he croaked, stepping out onto the verandah. Lyall and Saskia edged backwards.

'Sorry,' said Saskia. 'We didn't know anybody lived here.'

'What did you do to your leg?' asked Lyall.

'*Non sono affari tuoi!*' he said angrily, pointing one of his crutches towards Lyall as if it might have been a machine gun. 'And no dogs here, *capito? Niente cani.*'

'Sor-ry,' said Lyall. 'I was just trying to make conversation.

'You're Italian!' said Saskia. 'We're learning Italian at school, aren't we, Lyall?'

'*Sì,*' said Lyall. '*Il mio nome è Lyall, questo è Saskia e questo è Sunday.*' You could tell Lyall was dead proud of himself for being able to remember how to introduce himself in Italian. '*Come ti chiami?*' Lyall continued, which means *What's your name*, in Italian. Even I knew that.

'*Lasciatemi in pace!*' the man said and slammed the door as hard as he could in our faces.

'What sort of name is that?' I asked.

'He said, "Leave me in peace". In other words, *Rack off!*' said Lyall.

'Weird old rude mean man!' said Saskia.

Good one, Mum, I thought to myself. *Why didn't you tell*

*us there was a psychopath at the bottom of the garden? Granny's
house has been empty for months. Why is he still here?'*

After we'd explored absolutely every square inch of the
house and the garden, we all gathered in the kitchen where
Mum and Carl were sorting through boxes.

'Yum. What's cooking?' I asked.

'Lasagne,' Mum said. 'Carl made a couple of trays and
froze them before we moved, so we'd have something ready
on our first night.' Mum looked all goo-goo eyed at Carl,
as though he were the cleverest man on earth, and Carl
looked as if he agreed with Mum wholeheartedly.

'Yep – just need to make a salad,' he said.

Then they let us in on the news that although they'd
ordered our new beds weeks ago, the beds weren't going to
make it in time for our first night.

'It's not so bad,' said Carl. 'You guys can set up camp
in the games room. It will be a good opportunity to get to
know all the new noises and creaks the house makes.'

'Dad, why is it called a games room when there are no
games in it?' asked Saskia.

'There used to be a big billiard table,' said Mum. 'But
Granny sold it when *you-know-who* went away.' (I think
Mum was referring to Grandpa Henry.)

'Oh,' said Saskia. 'That's a shame.'

'So,' said Carl, 'have you three come to any kind of

arrangement about which bedrooms you'd like? I presume you all want to sleep upstairs?'

'Mum, when is the mean old dude in the cottage moving out?' I asked, hoping the precookeds weren't reading my mind as I thought about myself all tucked up in my new double bed up in the turret.

'His name is Settimio, Sunny,' said Mum, taking the newspaper wrapping off some wine glasses.

'Whatever. Why is he still here? Is it just because he can't move out till his leg gets better?'

Mum looked me straight in the eye. 'Settimio isn't going to be moving out I'm afraid, Sunny. Your grandmother gave him the cottage. He was her gardener for over forty years, you know. They were dear old friends. And it was Settimio, actually, who found Granny Carmelene the day she died, and phoned to let us know.'

'This is a disaster!' I said. 'Why didn't you tell me, Mum?'

'I'm sure you kids will soon get to know him,' said Carl. 'But maybe, for a little while, it might be worth keeping out of his way.'

'You know, Carl,' said Mum. 'I think we should just put all this stuff up in the attic. There's not one thing that this kitchen hasn't already got.'

'Sure, darl. I'm making a pile in the games room for attic-bound objects. Lyall, do us a favour and put these things in there, will you?'

'Sure, Dad,' said Lyall.

'And Sunny,' continued Carl. 'For the winter months at least, your job is to make sure there's plenty of firewood in the boxes in the library. You know where to get the wood from? There's a woodpile down near—'

'Near Settimio's! You just finished telling me to stay away from him! You guys are so confusing. It's no wonder the kids of today have issues.'

'Come on, Sunny,' said Carl. 'I said keep out of his way, which ultimately means keeping Willow from annoying him. She's not the easiest dog, now is she?'

Willow, asleep on the floor next to the heating panel, lifted her head momentarily when she heard Carl say her name.

'It's okay, Willow,' I said. 'I'm on your side.'

Granny Carmelene's kitchen had a dishwasher. (Not like at our old place, where the dishwasher happened to be me.) And there was a pantry you could walk right into, lined with jars of yummy preserved fruity things that hopefully we'd be having with ice-cream. Seriously, the pantry was so well stocked that if there ever were some type of war or famine we could survive for at least ten years without ever needing to leave the house.

I moved a few things around to make a good spot for Willow's big tin of dog pellets, then I helped Mum make a dressing for the salad, and even got to be the first one to use Granny Carmelene's whiz-bang salad spinner.

All without feeling the slightest bit sad. I had to hand it to Bruce and Terry. They really were top-rate bouncers.

I remembered the day Granny Carmelene and I had tea by the river, and that made me think of when I wagged school and Granny Carmelene and I had lunch at the Hopetoun Tea Rooms. But I didn't get *sad* one bit.

I just thought about the chocolate eclairs and the chilled chicken sandwiches and how Granny Carmelene let me go to the spell shop too.

All that got me thinking about Bruce and Terry. If they were that good, maybe they could also do something about Settimio.

5.

'**Bags the turret** bedroom! *Keepings off!*' Lyall yelled the next afternoon as soon as he saw our beds had been delivered.

We'd just got home from our first day of catching buses all the way across town to school. Before I could even yell out, *As if!* Saskia burst through the door too, and I nearly collided with her as I flew up the stairs two at a time.

Unfortunately for Willow, Mum stopped her from following us. Mum was talking about making upstairs a no-go zone for dogs (which we all knew would never work, but we had to let her at least try and then fail).

'Come on guys,' shouted Carl, as Saskia thumped up the stairs behind me. 'Remember what I said about seeing if you can come to some sort of *mutual* agreement!'

To be honest (and I do *try* to be honest these days), I felt like I *deserved* first choice of bedrooms. I mean, Granny Carmelene was *my* flesh and blood grandmother after all. Lyall and Saskia had never even met her. And if it wasn't for their dad latching onto my mum, and them being all tragically in love, and us becoming all modern and blended, Lyall and Saskia would still be living at their Mum's place, and I wouldn't have to be *one bit* community minded.

Luckily, I had a plan to make sure that everyone mutually agreed with me. Have you ever heard of Reverse Psychology? It's all about acting as though you're taking a stance about a particular something, while knowing that by *pretending*, you'll be actually encouraging another person (in this case, Lyall), to take the *opposite* stance. I could give you lots of impressive examples of Reverse Psychology but that would mean I'd be getting off the point so if you're really interested, try googling Tom Sawyer and see how he got all his friends to paint a fence.

I had to restrain myself from racing up into the turret after Lyall (because a key factor to being successful at Reverse Psychology is *nonchalance,* which basically means looking as though you don't really care – kind of like how Claud behaves when she likes a boy, not to mention her fake laughing). So I stopped on the second floor. Saskia walked into the big bedroom next to Granny Carmelene's old room. (Nobody was allowed to have Granny's room; it was going to be for guests, once we'd sorted it out.)

'I just *love* this room,' I said (white lie), standing by the window. 'Imagine waking up every morning and looking out at all those roses.'

'Me too,' said Saskia. 'This room is my absolute *favourite*.'

'Oh, really?' I said in a despondent way, looking disappointed. 'I kind of think it's a bit grown-up for you. And not very *arty*, if you know what I mean.'

Lyall burst through the door. 'Yep, the turret is definitely the room for me.' he said. 'It's a boy thing.'

'That's not fair!' whined Saskia. 'I might want the turret, or Sunny might. You got the best room at Mum's!' Saskia looked to me to back her up.

But instead I said, 'It's the perfect room for you, Lyall. Besides, I'd be too freaked out to sleep up there. Probably wouldn't get any sleep at all.'

'Why?' asked Lyall, still puffing.

'Yeah, Sunny,' said Saskia. '*Why?*'

'Oh nothing,' I said, in my best *nonchalant* voice. 'Just something Granny Carmelene told me, but it's probably not true. Anyway, all old houses have those freaky stories. Especially houses like this one, you know, with portraits that talk and all.'

'Eeew! Don't tell me any freaky stories. I want *this* room,' said Saskia, blocking her ears. 'I don't care if it's not arty.'

Lyall and I headed for the turret.

'Tell me, Sunny,' he said, as we made our way up the stairs. 'What did Granny Carmelene say to you about the turret room?'

I took my time to answer him, peering through the telescope and aiming it towards the high branches of the cypress tree.

'Tell me, Sunny!'

'Sorry? This thing sure is difficult to focus.'

'The *story*, Sunny. What did she tell you?'

'Oh, that.' I said turning away from the telescope to face Lyall. I dropped my voice down to a near whisper and leant in close. '*Bats*, Lyall. That'd be the story about *bats*.'

Lyall looked slightly disappointed.

'Apparently they circle the turret at night. Granny said they've even been known to smash through the windows. I guess 'cos they're in search of *blood*.'

'Get real, Sunny! We've got fruit bats in Australia. They're not after blood.'

My nose was practically touching Lyall's. 'You just don't get it, do you, Lyall? They're called *fruit* bats because they can smell the fruit *in your blood*. So you accidentally eat a few too many dried apricots, or you have a bit too much pineapple on your Hawaiian, maybe even just a bit too much juice... I tell you at *any* moment in the middle of the night a freaking *bat* could smash through your bedroom window. Not that it would effect you though,

Lyall. You hardly eat much fruit these days. You should *definitely* have the turret. I'm just letting you in on the deal, okay? Don't complain when it actually happens.' I pointed my finger at him, just like Terry does.

'*As if*, Sunny! What do you take me for?' said Lyall, holding his ground. 'Next thing you'll be telling me the word *gullible* has been taken out of the English dictionary.'

'*Really*? Has it?' I asked. 'Who told you that?'

Lyall laughed hysterically, and even punched my arm.

'Yeah right, Sunny! Talk about *gullible*!'

'I do believe we're having our first fight, Lyall,' I said, straight faced, to conceal my embarrassment. I held onto the throb in my arm where he had hit me, hoping my gullibility wouldn't affect this most critical stage of Reverse Psychology. 'Maybe you'd like to punch my other arm too, Lyall?' I said, hoping a little more nonchalance would get us back on track.

'What's so funny?' yelled Saskia from downstairs, which was perfect timing as I needed a reason to casually leave.

'I'll be there in a sec, Saskia!' I shouted back. You see, I was about to implement the *Walk Away*, which is the absolute key to making Reverse Psychology a success. Mind you, the Walk Away isn't easy. It takes solid commitment, because no matter how badly you might want something, you have to have the strength (and nonchalance) to simply turn your back and walk away.

'Okey-dokey then, I'm out of here,' I said, turning to go downstairs. 'I think I'll go for the room opposite Saskia's. It's a girl thing. It's also closer to the kitchen, 'cos I'm planning on *having* midnight feasts, not *being* one. I'll tell Carl to bring your bed up to the turret, shall I, Lyall?'

'I haven't *decided*, Sunny. We're finalising it at dinner, like Dad said.'

You've got to admit that's just the sort of answer someone would give who wasn't as keen as he had been when he started.

At dinner, when we were all sitting around one end of the kitchen table, Carl said, 'Well, I take it by the peace and quiet around here that you guys have made a decision?'

'I'm having the room overlooking the front garden!' said Saskia.

'And I'm having the one across the hall from Saskia,' said Lyall.

'Great,' said Mum. 'And you Sunny?'

'Well, I did want the one opposite Saskia, but since nobody wants the turret, I'm thinking I might go for that.'

Lyall gave me *the eyebrow* and said, 'What about the *bats*, Sunny?'

But I just gave him *the eyebrow* straight back and said, 'I used to think the turret was kind of spooky, but now I'm thinking it'd be pretty cool ...

6.

All that Reverse Psychology meant I had forgotten to collect the firewood for the library fireplace.

'Sunny, I'm sorry but you'll just have to go and get some now. It won't take long,' said Mum, screwing pages of old newspapers into balls. 'Saskia didn't have any trouble remembering to gather the kindling.'

'But it's *really* dark, Mum.'

'Well, perhaps that might help you remember next time, Sunny. Now go on. There's a head-torch in the laundry cupboard; you can use that.' Mum clapped her hands like some type of a school mistress, so I made a point of making my way out extra slowly, just in case the hand clap was something she was thinking of adopting.

I put the head torch on and adjusted the angle of the

lamp so that it threw a circle of light in front of me. The grass was already wet with dew as I made my way down to the woodshed. Willow circled around me. 'Stay close, Willow,' I said. 'It's cold and dark and we're not going for a walk, okay.'

Once the wheelbarrow came into view, Willow started barking furiously and growling as though it was some type of strange animal.

'Shhh, Willow! It's just a wheelbarrow, silly,' I said. 'Come here and sit.'

But she continued barking and pacing so she'd be ready to pounce the moment it started moving. Meanwhile, I stacked it full of logs from the top of the pile. I clicked my fingers next to my side and Willow did a wide arc around the wheelbarrow and sat up tall next to me so I could give her a pat.

'Good girl,' I said bending down a little to reach her. 'You're such a funny dog, Willow. You don't like the big mean wheelbarrow at all do you. You're just a—'

'*That dog no good!*'

'Jeez!' I yelled, turning around to see Settimio's feet right behind me. I adjusted my lamp until it shone square in his face. 'Do you always go around sneaking up on people? You frightened the heck out of me *and* Willow '

Willow barked at him, because dogs are really good at sensing bad people, even if her next step in dealing with the bad person is usually to bolt and leave me alone to possibly get murdered.

Settimio leant back on one of his crutches, freeing the other one to wave about in a warding-off kind of way, towards Willow.

'No dogs here. Dogs no here. *Understand?*' Settimio actually roared. All the veins in his neck throbbed out and even his bald patch had gone red with rage. Willow hid behind me and buried her nose in the back of my knees. I glanced over my shoulder to see if anyone might be watching from the house, but I was completely out of view.

'Come on, Willow,' I said calmly, making sure I had hold of her collar. I turned back towards the house. 'We'll come back for the wood later. *With Carl*,' I shouted backwards at Settimio.

'You keep that dog tied up. *Comprendere?*'

We were almost at the back steps when I heard Settimio call out, 'You keep dog away or you be sorry, little girl! You be very sorry!'

I double-checked that neither Mum nor Carl were in the kitchen or anywhere in earshot. Then I yelled at the top of my voice, 'You're a mean old man, Settimio, and do you want to know what's worse? You've got hairs growing out of your ears! Understand? HAIRS!'

Willow cowered, as if she thought perhaps I was angry with her.

'It's all right, girl,' I said. 'You just stay away from him a while, okay?' I ushered Willow inside and slammed the back door as hard as I could behind me, even though Settimio was probably deaf and wouldn't be able to hear me.

'Well, thanks, Mum,' I said, safely back inside. 'Settimio creeps around in the night and who knows what else. I couldn't even get the wood because he frightened me so much, and he said Willow has to be tied up or else I'll be sorry. That's a threat Mum, a *threat*! And I'm going to make a note of it because I bet he does heaps more creepy stuff, and in the end the police are going to be asking all sorts of questions about Settimio, and I'll be able to tell them the exact times and the exact dates because I'll have a creep-list about ten miles long, and I wouldn't be surprised if he broke his leg doing something completely wrong-town like stealing people's washing and—'

'Calm down, Sunny,' Mum said. 'Settimio has every right to be out in his own garden, and I doubt very much his intention was to sneak up on you, darling.'

'Yeah, well, I don't want wood-collecting to be my job anymore.'

'I'll put the kettle on,' said Carl. 'Maybe you'd like a chamomile tea?'

'No thanks, Carl,' I said. 'It's my first night in my new room. I kind of want to make the most of it.'

7.

I couldn't possibly list all the good words that described my first night up in the turret. Apart from the word *victory* of course.

The *only* problem (besides the possibility of a bat through the window – ha ha, as if) was that because of the all-around, curtainless windows I was early-bird awake at the first light of day. I lay there and looked at all the parts of my official new bedroom, which didn't take too long on account of it being a rather small room. The ceiling was all panelled and slanty with white painted boards and there were shelves built right around the doorway, where I'd already unpacked my books and ornaments. On my bedside table I had two lamps: my old lighthouse lamp that Dad gave me for my second birthday and my hippie lava-lamp that Auntie Guff gave me when I turned ten. The lava-lamp was impossible to read by, but perfect for creating atmosphere. When it was on, the whole room glowed dusky pink and I felt like I was inside a genie bottle.

Outside, the sky was white with fog and clouds, but I was all snuggled up in my new double bed, like a bird in a nest. That's when I had the idea to spy on Settimio with Granny Carmelene's telescope. I mean, what else was there to do at that hour? I leapt out of bed, pulled off the lens cap and swung the telescope towards Settimio's cottage and twisted the focus to home in on the window that faced the turret. Would you believe I could see straight into Settimio's kitchen? I could see him making coffee and reading the paper. I could even see what paper he was reading. It was all written in Italian.

Suddenly I felt a bit guilty, which should have been a signal for me to stop, but with Settimio being a confirmed dog-hater and all, I kind of felt entitled. Just then, Settimio stood up from the kitchen table in his huge old-man underpants. And I mean huge. It was enough to put me off spying forever. At least until after breakfast.

Mum was already up. 'Here she is,' she said, as I walked into the kitchen. 'How did you sleep in your new big bed? Were you warm enough up there?' She gave me a kiss on the side of the head.

'Warm as toast, thanks, Mum,' I said, looking about for Willow. She wasn't keeping warm by the heater panel. 'Where's Willow?' I asked.

'Oh, I haven't seen her this morning,' said Mum. 'I presumed she'd snuck upstairs with you.'

I ran and opened the back door. 'Willow!' I called. '*Willow!*'

It was freezing outside. There was no way she'd be out there for long by herself. Maybe she was curled up with Lyall or Saskia? I went to the bottom of the stairs and called out, but she didn't come.

'I wouldn't worry about it too much, Sunny.' Mum said. 'She'll show up. She's probably just off exploring. You know what she's like when she's chasing a scent. Deaf as a mute. At any rate, you better have some breakfast and get a move on or you'll miss the bus.

Mum spooned some hot porridge into a bowl and put it on the table in front of me, and I poured on way too much honey and quickly mixed it in while she had her back turned making the lunches. I could hear Lyall and Saskia thumping about upstairs.

'Come on, you two!' Carl called up the stairs. 'If you want a lift to school we have to get moving! Oh, morning, Sunny,' he said, looking about for the coffee Mum had poured him.

'Morning, Carl. Have you seen Willow anywhere?'

'Not since last night, now you come to mention it,' said Carl

'Mum, can you text me when Willow turns up. Otherwise I'll be worried all day.'

'Sure, sweetheart. I'll be here trying to get my workspace set up. I've got clients this afternoon and the place is still so disorganised.'

Living so far from school all of a sudden sure meant having longer wintry mornings. I was standing at the bus stop in my brand new red fingerless gloves, puffing out dragon breath and thinking how if we were still living in Elwood, I could lie in bed until a quarter to nine and still get to school on time. Luckily, it was only going to be until the end of the year that I would have to take the bus, and soon it would be holidays anyway.

I pulled my favourite old stripy socks as far as possible over my sticky-outy knees. The rest of my legs were goosebumpy blotches of pink, blue and red. I wouldn't blame you if you're wondering why I didn't wear long pants (or woolly tights at least) instead of a short denim skirt and a hoodie. It's a wonder Mum let me out the door at all. I guess she knew that insisting I wear something warmer and actually *finding* something warmer were two very different things. We were still rummaging through boxes to find everything from the remote control to a pair of jeans.

I was trying my best not to worry about Willow, and to make matters worse, the bus was so crowded that I had to worry standing up. I tried to distract myself by thinking about the school holidays and how I was going to be spending more time with Flora over at Dad and Steph's.

To cheer myself away from thinking something horrible might have happened to Willow, I thought of all the cutest things about Flora. That's when I noticed there was a spare seat next to some random boy knitting a scarf. I squeezed in next to him and pushed my bag under the seat in front.

'Oh no!' he said, as a whole row of stitches slipped clean off one of his needles. 'Don't move.'

'Sorry,' I said sheepishly, watching him follow the line of wool down to my bag and unhook it from the zipper. 'It must have just latched on.'

'Don't worry about it,' he said, carefully threading each dropped stitch back onto the needle. 'I think I got them all.'

'Cool scarf,' I said. 'I love everything stripy.'

'I noticed,' he said, looking down at my socks. Then he read the label on my school bag. 'Sunny Hathaway, huh?'

'As in Sunday.' I said, not really knowing what to say next. Asking what his name was just seemed so tit-for-tat.

'My dog's missing,' I said, at exactly the same moment that he said, 'I'm Finn,' and held out his hand for me to shake.

'Hi, Finn,' I said, right at the same time that he said, 'That's awful. What sort of dog is it?'

I suddenly wondered if it was bad manners to shake someone's hand while wearing fingerless gloves, but considering Finn was a knitter, maybe it was okay.

'I'm Sunny,' I said. 'I mean, you know that already, sorry.'

'I do,' said Finn, packing his knitting in his back-pack and standing up to press the button for the next stop.

'What I meant was: she's a greyhound. Willow's a greyhound.' I was wondering what school he went to, but before I could ask he said, 'Rudolph Steiner. And you?'

'Elwood Primary. We just moved,' I said, knowing he was wondering why I'd be going to a school so far away. 'I'm finishing the year off at my old school.'

The bus slowed down and pulled over at Finn's stop. 'Have you checked your old place, Sunny? Maybe Willow's there. She might still think it's home. Dogs do that sometimes, you know.'

'Brilliant idea! I'll check our old place,' I said, wondering why I hadn't thought of that myself.

'See you, Sunny,' he said, making his way to the door. 'I hope you find your dog.'

'Thanks,' I said. 'Nice to meet you, Finn.'

The bus doors folded shut and I waved to Finn as he walked past my window. That's when the strangest feeling hit the pit of my stomach. The only way I can describe it is

47

that when I'd woken up that morning Finn hadn't existed, but by the time I got to school, he not only existed, but out of nowhere, he suddenly *mattered*. Maybe it was the knitting? It's possible.

But seriously, what if I had the beginnings of a crush? A pre-crush? No! After seeing how weird Claud went over Buster Conroy I swore it would never happen to me. Claud's laugh turned so fake you could practically spell it.

But even a possible pre-crush wasn't enough to stop me worrying about Willow. I worried all through Science and all through Maths, and I worried a whole lot more through RE. I checked my phone at recess but there was no message from Mum. At lunch I called her.

'Nothing yet I'm afraid, sweetheart,' said Mum apologetically.

'Have you asked Settimio?'

'I did, Sunny, and apart from him telling me Willow had chased poor old Marmalade under the house again, he said he hadn't seen her since yesterday. I don't want you to worry too much. She'll be back for dinner, I'm sure.'

'What if she's trying to walk back to our old place, Mum? Dogs do that you know. There're so many busy roads, and you know how hopeless she is in traffic, and what if she gets—'

'Try not to think the worst, Sunny. If she's wandering about, someone will find her and give us a call. Trust me, she'll be okay. She's smarter than she looks, you know.'

Just to be certain, I went back to our old place after school. I was hoping she'd be lying exhausted under the fig tree, just like old times. I could fully understand Willow thinking our old place was still her home; it still felt like my home too. I could have walked on in and dumped my bag in the hall, just like I always used to.

The new people had already put up a weird temporary carport made of canvas, like you see in caravan parks. It felt like such an intrusion. There was no car under it though, so I felt safe that the intruders weren't home. I clicked open the gate, almost expecting Willow to fly down the side of the house with her tail whipping about like a propeller.

But there was nothing.

I really wanted to sneak down the side and see what the new people had done to the shed, but I didn't, because I had no right to be there any more. That house was the most familiar place in the world to me, but suddenly it was out-of-bounds.

I had written a note in RE, asking the new people to call if Willow showed up, and I slipped it under their door hoping they didn't have a pet who might eat it. Then I ran to the bus stop as fast as humanly possible. I looked at my watch. I had been worrying about Willow for nine solid hours.

The whole way home on the bus I practised the positive

49

visualisation techniques that Auntie Guff had taught me. I closed my eyes and imagined seeing Willow's snout under the gate when I got home. Then I imagined her jumping all over me. I even let her tear my sock and I didn't get cross. I imagined Willow so hard I could almost smell her.

But when I walked up our street there was no Willow-snout pressed under the gate and no Willow jumping all over me, or doing laps of the house. There was no trace of Willow at all. The front garden was as quiet and still as that first day I'd visited Granny Carmelene, way back when I hadn't even met her yet and didn't even know she was going to die.

'W–i–l–l–o–w!' I called, closing the gate behind me. When she didn't come, the pink rubber ends of my vast balloon of hope slipped from my grasp, and I watched it make frantic balloon circles in the air before falling limply to the ground.

It's Settimio, I thought. *He's done something to her. I just know it.*

I stomped straight around the back of the house towards Settimio's cottage. I knew he was home, because apart from the fact that he never went anywhere, I could see smoke coming from his chimney. I threw my school bag down at his gate, marched down his cobblestone path and thumped on his door with two flat hands. I could hear him hobbling towards the door. When he opened it, he was wearing only a flannel shirt and a woollen vest over his bare plaster-cast legs. I'm sure he was dressed like that just to frighten me.

'What have you done with Willow!' I could feel my nostrils flaring and I was trying my hardest to stay angry so that I wouldn't cry.

'I already tell your mother,' said Settimio. 'I not see your *stupido* dog.' He tried to close the door in my face, but I stopped it with my foot.

'Go away!' he growled.

'Tell me where she is!' I yelled, but he closed the door hard against my foot and pushed the end of one crutch right on top of it until I had to pull it out of the way. Then I heard the door locking. I thumped on it with both hands.

'We're going to call the police, Settimio! *The police!*' I wished I knew the word for police in a language other than Indonesian. But I threw the Indonesian version at him all the same, just to make it sound like I was *really* serious. '*Polisi!*'

Then I ran to our back steps, almost tripping over my own school bag on the way. I stopped and yelled back towards Settimio's cottage as loud as I could: '*Dognapper!*'

I burst into tears the moment I got inside.

'Is that you, Sunday?' Mum called out from the kitchen.

I could smell dinner cooking, and it sure smelt like something meaty-cheesy-delicious, even if I wasn't going

51

to be feeding any to Willow under the table.

'I've been trying to call you for the last hour,' Mum said giving me a hug. 'Oh, Sunny, you've got yourself all worked up.'

Before she could say anything else, I heard a Willow-whine coming from the laundry, followed by some familiar snorting noises under the door. It was at that moment that I remembered the little voice I'd ignored when I'd arrived home and marched straight over to Settimio's. The little voice that told me to go inside and see Mum first.

'Apparently she took herself for a bit of a stroll by the river,' Mum said. 'Someone called me from Dights Falls!' She opened the laundry door and I dropped to my knees so that I would be on the right level for a Willow hug, which turned out to be impossible because Willow was so happy to see me it was all I could do to fend her off. She jumped and licked and wagged her tail so hard it was painful to hear it bang against the door. Then she pounced on my feet with her claws as I tried to stand up.

'Come on, Willow, settle down,' I said, but she took off down the hall, racing in and out of the dining room, in and out of the drawing room and the library, then up and down the hall again.

'Seems she may have missed you, Sunny,' said Mum. 'She's been searching for you for the last hour and a half. I had to put her bed by the heater in the laundry just so I could get the dinner on.'

'Oh dear,' I said, as Willow ran back towards me and buried her snout between my knees. I was feeling dreadful about what I'd said to Settimio. And especially silly for the Indonesian police part. 'What was I thinking?' I said under my breath.

'Sunday?'

'Oh, it's nothing, Mum. Just a little misunderstanding.'

'With who?'

'Settimio. I kind of accused him of being involved with Willow's disappearance. But you've got to admit, Mum, it really did look that way. He threatened me remember?'

'Mmmm,' said Mum looking sceptical. 'Sounds to me like *someone* owes Settimio an apology.'

'Aw, come on, Mum. I was traumatised. He's probably already forgotten.'

But Mum gave me *the eyebrow*, as if to say, *You'll apologise, Sunny Hathaway, and that's that.*

8.

'Dad,' said Saskia at breakfast the next morning, 'how do you catch dyslexia?'

Lyall made a snorting noise into his porridge, and I could see Carl was trying his best to keep a straight face.

'Dyslexia's not something you *catch*, love. It's a genetic thing.'

'Oh,' said Saskia, disappointed.

Mum was packing three sets of school lunches. 'Now, Lyall, you will *eat* the banana won't you? There's no point just taking it to school for an outing and bringing it home again.'

'Oh no, I'll definitely, like, eat it, Alex. I promise.' Lyall said. 'Dad can we join the DVD library tonight and rent some movies? Last day of school and all.'

'Which reminds me, Mum, I said. 'We've got our class break-up party at lunch, so I won't need a sandwich.'

'Sunny, that's the sort of information that might have been useful *last night*.'

'I'll take it, darl, I love a packed lunch,' said Carl.

'Can I see if Claud can come for a sleepover, Mum? Please, she's dying to visit.'

'Sure,' said Mum.

'So if you're not born with dyslexia you can't get it then?' said Saskia, putting her bowl in the dishwasher.

'Why would you *want* dyslexia, Saskia?' said Lyall, munching on toast.

'Hey, did you hear the one about the dyslexic devil worshipper?' Carl looked thrilled to have yet another joke that he obviously felt was perfect for the occasion.

'Dad-uh!' said Saskia impatiently. 'I'm not—'

'He sold his soul to Santa!'

No one laughed, except for Carl and Mum. And I could tell she was just trying to be nice.

'Well, I want to be dyslexic because it means you're better at art and probably also a genius. Leonardo da Vinci was dyslexic,' said Saskia.

'You're already good at art, Saskia. It's your thing.' I said.

'Picasso was dyslexic. Andy Warhol was dyslexic. Albert Einstein was dys—'

'If you lot want a lift to school you'd better get a move

:d Carl, looking at his watch.

iise is dyslexic,' Saskia continued.

said Mum. 'I thought being a Scientologist
ough.'

'Thanks, Carl, but I think I'll take the bus,' I said.

'Why?' asked Lyall.

'No reason,' I said.

'Kiera Knightly's dyslexic. Orlando Bloom's dyslexic.
Cher, John Lennon, Richard Branson, Muhammad Ali.'

'Okay, okay, Saskia, we get the picture,' said Lyall
heading off to brush his teeth.

'*Agatha Christie was dyslexic!*' Saskia yelled after him.

Finn was on the bus knitting again.

There was even a spare seat next to him, so I sat down,
being careful not to get tangled up in his wool and hoping
like crazy that having a pre-crush wasn't an obvious-
looking thing.

'It's Sunny Hathaway,' Finn said. 'Hello. Did you find
your dog?'

I thought it was really decent that Finn remembered
about Willow. But then again that could have been the pre-
crush at work. Apparently, pre-crushes can make normal
little things about a person seem super-special.

'Hi, Finn,' I said. 'I did find my dog, thanks. She'd taken
herself on a bit of an adventure. What's your surname, Finn?'

'Fletcher-Lomax.'

'What sort of a surname is that?'

'The sort that's half my mum's surname and half my dad's.'

I hoped I hadn't sounded rude. I mean, it's not as if every third kid at school doesn't have a double-barrelled surname. And it's not that Mum says they're super-pretentious. It's more that I worry about all the quadruple-barrelled names in future generations. Has anyone actually thought it through? You could end up with a surname like Fletcher-Lomax-Aristotle-Percival-Garfield-Fotherington-Smythe. Or will there just be one generation of people with double-barrelled surnames, just like how there's a definite generation of people with names like Edna, Percy and Dot? Can you imagine *anyone* calling a little baby Edna any more?

I was way down a tangent but Finn pulled me out of it. 'You on MSN?' he asked.

'Yep.'

'MySpace?'

'Sure, you?'

'Don't have a computer,' said Finn, taking a felt-covered rainbow-coloured notebook from his bag. 'Here, write down your snail-mail address.' He passed me a pencil, rolled his knitting into a ball and stabbed it with the spare needle to keep it in place. Then he pushed the button for his stop and squeezed past me into the aisle.

'Are you having a party or something?' I asked, wondering why on earth he'd need my address. 'I'll put my phone number on too.'

'Don't have a phone,' said Finn. 'I'll explain later.'

I finished scribbling down our address, closed the notebook and handed it back to him.

'You around for the hols, Sunny Hathaway?'

'Yep,' I said. 'I'll be unpacking boxes, unfortunately.' I was thinking of all that cardboard I'd have to handle.

'Well, you'll be hearing from me,' he said. Finn stepped down from the bus and the doors folded shut behind him.

I turned in my seat and looked over my shoulder to the foggy exhaust of the back window as the bus groaned its way back into the traffic. Pre-crush or not I could sure do with a friend who lived on my side of town. Especially a friend who went to another school and who absolutely nobody else knew. A girl needs a friend all to herself, I tell you. Maybe Finn could be the new model Claud?

9.

When I got to school, Buster and Claud were sitting over by the basketball court. Buster was eating pieces of cooked sausage out of a tartan thermos with a pair of chopsticks. He must have noticed me giving him *the eyebrow*.

'What?' he said. 'It's the only way I can reach the bits down the bottom.'

'Fair enough,' said Claud, who thought absolutely *anything* Buster said or did was *fair enough* these days, even eating chopped-up sausages out of a drinking vessel first thing in the morning.

'I forgot about the class party for lunch,' Buster said. 'So I'm having lunch now, which is kind of good 'cos I missed breakfast. Want some, Sunny?' he said, holding a chunk of steamy sausage towards me. 'There's sauce down the bottom, if you want to dip it back in.'

'Ah, no thanks, Buster, I've got a tummy full of porridge.'

At lunch-time all the Year Sixes met in the kitchen area next to the hall for our mid-year break-up party. The windows were all steamed up from the smell of frankfurts, cuppa-soup and party-pies. There was also a slight foot-odour smell, but I shouldn't talk about that right when I'm talking about lunch.

Miranda Percival's mum had come to help and was buttering a bag of hot-dog rolls. 'Going anywhere for the holidays, Sunday?' Mrs Percival said as I stood in line for a cup of cordial.

'Not these hols,' I said, suddenly remembering that we hadn't really been anywhere last holidays either and that if it became a pattern I had every right to put in a complaint to Mum *and* Dad, in which case there was every chance I could end up getting *two* holidays. It was another up-side to divorce.

'We're going skiing,' said Miranda pushing in next to me.

'Do you ski, Sunny?' asked Mrs Percival in an ever-so-sensitive voice, as if not skiing might be a reason to call the Kids Help Line.

'We snowboard don't we, Sunny?' said Claud, butting in.

Claud was going away for the holidays too. She and her brother Walter were booked in to some horse-riding camp. Even Buster was heading up north on a trip with his mum. Could this mean that my only company for the school hols was destined to be the precookeds? Just as Mrs Percival handed me a hot dog I lost my appetite.

'Thank you,' I said, moving over to join the huddle by the heater and looking around for Buster in case I needed someone to eat my hot dog for me. Buster will eat practically anything.

But then I remembered Finn, and the way he called me *Sunny Hathaway*, and how he had said to me on the bus, *you'll be hearing from me,* and how I really hoped I would.

At that moment I knew the pre-crush was official. After just two meetings. If that was the case, I'd have to get my head around ignoring him, becuase everyone knows it's the first thing you do when you actually like someone.

Buster ended up sleeping over as well as Claud. Mum and Carl made risotto and we hired a pile of DVDs for a movie night in the gameless games room. At least there was a TV in there now and Mum had bought some beanbags too, so it was kind of a rumpus room just for us kids.

Buster was pretty quiet during dinner, but as soon as Mum and Carl had snuck off to the library he said, 'Gee, Sunny, if I'd known your Granny was filthy rich I wouldn't have cried so much at her funeral.'

'That's ridiculous, Buster. Everyone knows money doesn't *really* make people happy.'

'Rich people sure *look* happy,' he said. 'What's there to be unhappy about?'

'Well, being rich didn't prevent Granny Carmelene from having a big fat disease, Buster. Have you thought about that?'

'I'd still rather be rich and sick than poor and sick, Sunny.'

'How 'bout rich and dead, Buster? Do you really think being rich helps when you're dead? You're seriously deranged.'

Claud gave me a crinkled look as if to say, *Chill, Sunny, there's no need to get so upset.*

But I *was* upset, and if I'd known Buster was going to make me have sad thoughts about Granny Carmelene, I never would have agreed to have him over. And where were Bruce and Terry when I needed them? I needed some *Woe-Be-Gone* grief repellent quick smart.

'Does anyone want a hot chocolate?' asked Saskia.

I could tell she was looking for an excuse to leave the room, and Claud obviously had the same idea.

'Yum,' said Claud, 'I'll help you make it. Come on, Sunny. Show us where everything's kept. You guys stay here. We'll be back soon.' Claud was acting all embarrassed, as if Buster's stupid comments were somehow *her* fault, and once we were in the kitchen she said, 'Sorry Sunny, it's just that he's—'

'Forget it, Claud,' I said, passing her the cocoa and the sugar from out of the pantry. 'I'd rather talk about something else.' That's when I noticed Bruce and Terry standing in the shadows down the back of the pantry.

'Psst! Close the door a minute, Sunny,' Terry said.

I flicked a glance over to Claud and Saskia, who were busy getting cups out and heating milk on the stove, and I quietly slid the door closed. Bruce held the can of grief repellent high above my head.

'Close your eyes,' he said, and I immediately felt the soothing mist settle over me. 'Now, scram!' he said, as Terry slid open the door for me.

'Claud, did you know there's a high chance I might be dyslexic?' said Saskia, stirring the milk.

Claud gave her *the eyebrow*. 'Ah, no, Sunny didn't tell me.'

'It's because I'm so good at art,' said Saskia, as though it was the most obvious thing on earth. 'Isn't it, Sunny?'

I was looking about for Granny's old autotray (a trolley on wheels) so we could wheel our hot chocolates back and join the others.

'Oh, there it is,' I said, ignoring Saskia's question and removing a pile of newspapers from the top of the trolley. 'Did you put enough sugar in, Claud? That cocoa is bitter as.' As I was taste-testing further with a teaspoon I realised just how potent Bruce and Terry's grief repellent actually was. I was completely cured, I tell you. Cured.

After the movie we all scrambled up to the turret. Claud and I were in my bed while Buster, Lyall and Saskia each had a sleeping bag and a sleeping mat and sardined themselves on the floor. Then we set about spooking ourselves with scary stories until Buster had to go and ruin it all by telling a *true* one. It was about two Goths on the Sandringham train and how one of them was propped up against the other one like she might be feeling sick or something, but it turned out the leaning over one was actually dead, and the holding-her-up one actually had a knife.

Saskia started crying. 'Now I'm never going to be able to catch a train again,' she sobbed, and we all looked at Lyall as if to say, *She's your responsibility, dude.*

'Come on,' said Lyall, 'I'll take you downstairs to Dad and Alex.'

'Sorry,' said Buster. 'I thought everyone had heard that one.'

'I'm only nine, you know, Buster!' Saskia yelled back at him on her way out. Then she started crying again. I could tell being *only nine* didn't mean that much to Buster.

'Talk about sensitive!' he said to Claud, rolling his eyes.

Talk about insensitive! I thought to myself.

By the next afternoon I was a little 'peopled out'. So it was perfect timing that I was heading off to Dad and Steph's.

Also, I couldn't wait to see Flora. I really do miss her when I'm not around. Don't get me wrong, I miss Dad and Steph too. It's just that being only five months old and my real little baby half-sister, Flora is way cuter than anything else in my world, even Willow's puppy photos.

I left Claud and Buster up in the turret, taking turns with the telescope and possibly pashing, and went to see how lunch was going. With Buster around all the time, I hadn't even had a chance to tell Claud about Finn.

'I'll call you guys when it's ready,' I said as I thumped down the narrow stairs. I was so hungry my stomach growled.

Mum and Carl were in the kitchen doing – wait for it – *the crossword*. Even sadder than having parental figures who are addicted to crosswords is having parental figures who are addicted to *cryptic crosswords*. At least with the Quick I could sometimes help. Seriously, besides making new rules and rosters every five seconds, cryptic crossword clues are practically all Mum and Carl ever talk about, and believe me, they make no sense at all.

'Oh, that's an easy one,' said Mum, as Carl took a pie out of the oven. 'Fifteen down. *Stars tell how horrors manage – it's horoscope.*'

'Good work, love,' said Carl peering over Mum's shoulder. 'So what does that make eighteen across now? Fourth letter is 'r'. *Scorched salt water crimson.*'

'Looks delicious,' I said. 'What is it?'

'Hunza pie,' said Carl. 'Made completely from the vegetable garden.'

'Oh,' I said, hoping to hide my disappointment. I could hear Saskia coming in the back door.

'Are we ever going to *eat*?' she asked, still puffing from running around with Willow, who gulped down half a bowl of water before collapsing on the floor under the table.

'Yeah, Mum,' I said. 'You know, *eat* – three letters, what growing children need to do three times a day?'

'All right, Sunny,' said Mum, putting the newspaper aside. 'No need to be sarcastic. Why don't you go and find Lyall and help set the table.'

'I'll get him!' said Saskia. She darted out into the entrance hall, stood at the base of the stairs and yelled '*L-y-y-y-y-a-a-ll, l-u-u-u-u-nch!*' at the top of her voice. Then she came back into the kitchen, still short of breath, and said, 'Settimio told me off. Sunny's right. He *is* mean.'

I could hear Lyall thumping down the stairs.

'That reminds me, Sunny,' said Carl. 'Have you apologised to Settimio yet?'

I glared at Saskia for being the one to remind him. 'Not yet,' I said. 'But not now, I've got friends over.'

Mum and Carl gave each other *the eyebrow*, and Mum pointed towards the back door and said, 'Now, Sunny.

You'll be off to your dad and Steph's soon. Do it now, please.'

'That pie smells *so* good,' said Lyall appearing in the kitchen. 'What was Settimio saying to you, Saskia? I could see you out my window?'

'It's Willow,' said Saskia. 'She's dug up all his artichokes and chased Marmalade again. He said Marmalade is *too old* and might *have heart attack.*' Saskia was mimicking Settimio and his Italian accent. 'Then, he poked me in the leg with one of his crutches.'

'*Now*, Sunny.' Mum took me by the shoulders, turned me around from where I was getting some cutlery out of the drawer, faced me in the direction of the door and gave me a gentle push. 'Go and apologise for your outburst the other day, *and* promise him you'll get Willow under control.'

I deposited the bunch of knives and forks I was holding in a pile on the table. ''Kay' I said, looking about to see if anyone would come with me. Lyall and Saskia became suddenly frantic about setting the table. Even Willow pretended she was asleep.

'*Now*, Sunny!' Mum and Carl barked in unison.

All the way over to the cottage I was rehearsing my lines. *Sorry, Settimio, bye. Sorry, Settimio, that you really are the biggest grump alive. I'm sorry, Settimio, that you hate animals and children. Sorry about your hairy ears, Settimio.*

Sorry I yelled at you, but it sure felt good, Settimio. See ya, wouldn't wanna be ya, Settimio!

Before I knew it, I was knocking on his door and he was on the other side opening it.

'Hello, Settimio,' I said politely. 'I just wanted to say that I'm sorry for yelling at you the other day. I was very worried about Willow, who I know annoys you and that's another reason I'm sorry, and I'm going to make sure she doesn't do any more bad things like chasing Marmalade. So yeah – that's pretty much it. Sorry. Bye.' I'd been looking at his feet the whole time. When my eyes finally met his, I noticed they were all weepy looking. *Oh no*, I thought. *I've made Settimio cry.*

Then he slammed the door in my face.

As I was walking back to the house I thought about how it sure felt bad to apologise and have someone *still* be upset with you. I mean, I'd done my bit, wasn't he meant to say, *That's okay?*

'Well done, Sunny,' said Mum. 'How did it go?' She had one of those patronising looks on her face. Kind of a mixture of *Good girl* and *I told you so.*

'Well, I apologised, but he's still down on me, so what can I do?'

'Oh, Sunny,' said Mum. 'He'll come around. It's early days.'

Carl had cut the pie into eight pieces and Lyall was

68

using the cake slide to lift them onto each plate.

'I've been thinking,' Lyall said, 'and I've got an idea that could really help Willow stay out of trouble.'

'Look out,' taunted Saskia. 'Lyall's been *thinking*.'

'Where're Claud and Buster?' I said, suddenly realising I had forgotten to call them for lunch.

'Still up in the turret, I think,' Saskia said. 'I'll go call them!'

She was halfway to the door when Carl intercepted. 'Oh no you won't, young lady. You have to stop screaming up and down those stairs.'

'Don't worry,' said Lyall, pulling his phone out of his pocket. 'I'll send Buster an SMS.'

'You'll do nothing of the sort,' said Carl. 'Sunny, would you mind using your *legs* and going upstairs to tell your friends that lunch is ready?'

'Sure,' I said, thinking that Lyall's text idea wasn't such a bad one and that I'd probably do it myself if my phone wasn't permanently out of credit.

I made lots of noise thumping up the turret stairs, just in case Claud and Buster actually *had* been pashing all that time. But they were just lounging around on the floor looking at stuff on Buster's laptop.

'Lunch, you guys,' I said.

'Yay!' said Claud, and they both sprang to their feet and took off downstairs.

I picked up my pillows from the floor and threw them back on the bed. That's when I noticed the lens cap from the telescope dangling on its string and went to put it back in place. Don't ask me *why* I thought it would be a good idea to have a quick snoop on Settimio. It just seemed to happen automatically. I lined up the telescope towards his cottage and pulled it into focus at the kitchen window.

He was right there at the table. I couldn't see the whole of him, but I could see his hands going through papers in an old shoe box. I focused a little closer. There were photographs and old coins, a couple of smaller tin boxes and letters in old-looking envelopes. Maybe that was why he looked all misty and weepy. He'd been making himself sad by being sentimental and all memory-lanesy.

Why do people do that? Keep a whole lot of old stuff that makes them feel all bent out of shape? I just don't get it. It's kind of just as weird as people (like Mum) who actually *like* movies that make them cry. Still, it was kind of reassuring to know that it wasn't me who'd made him cry. I'd obviously caught him in a bad moment.

When I got downstairs the others had started eating without me.

'What took you so long?' asked Claud.

'Nothing, really, just straightened up a bit.' I reached over for some tomato relish to help disguise the fact that the hunza pie was so full of vegies. 'What's your idea about anyway, Lyall?' I asked.

'Well,' he said, with a mouth full of pie. 'It's a dog entertaining business. We can set up all sorts of activities in the garden and get paid to entertain neighbourhood dogs after school and on holidays, while people are at work. I thought we could call it *Boredom Control*. What do you think?'

'Um, it's ah...*interesting*,' I said. 'Worth thinking about.'

'You sure do have plenty of room for it,' said Claud.

'Yeah, *stacks*,' added Buster.

'Can I design the brochures? asked Saskia.

Everybody looked over to me and gave me *the eyebrow*, all at the same time.

The thing was, ever since we'd moved I'd been trying to think of new business ideas. I really did like Lyall's idea, don't get me wrong. It's that just being an inventor and an entrepreneur, *I* should have been the one to think of it myself. I mean, if we did do Boredom Control and it was Lyall's idea, wouldn't that mean he was the boss? Can you imagine how tragic life would be if I had to take orders from a precooked? That would be about as wrong-town as you could get.

I glanced around the table to find everyone still looking at me.

'Sure,' I finally said. 'Let's do it. But you're not the boss of me, okay, Lyall? No one is.'

10.

'I don't know what the matter is,' said Steph tearily, after changing Flora's nappy. 'She's fed; she's changed; she's burped. I've been cuddling her all day.'

'Here,' said Dad, reaching for Flora. 'Sunny and I will take her for a walk in the pram. We'll get some groceries and fix dinner too, won't we, Sunny?'

'We'd better take this,' I said, holding up Flora's dummy as Dad lay her in the pram. She had stopped crying momentarily. I brushed the rubbery dummy gently against Flora's lips until she opened her mouth and sucked it in, making the cutest slurping noises, just like Maggie from *The Simpsons*.

'Try and get some rest, Steph,' said Dad, putting his arm around her. 'You look exhausted.' He kissed her on the

73

side of her forehead, which made her even tearier.

'Do you know the *worst* thing you can say to someone who's tired, James?' snapped Steph. Dad stared at her blankly. 'That they *look* tired!' And she stomped into the laundry, slamming the door behind her.

Dad looked at me guiltily. 'Come on, Sunny, grab the shopping list and we'll give Steph some peace.'

Steph slamming the door like that jangled my nerves and made me feel as though I shouldn't be there at all. Kind of like the time I was at Ruby's house and she got in trouble for exploding the microwave by heating the left-over spaghetti Bolognese with the tin foil still on. I just wanted to disappear. Which is when my imaginary aeroplane seat 44K comes in handy. Way up in the clouds, strung-out stepmothers and bad feelings don't seem to exist at all. I think it's something to do with the altitude. And also due to the fact that when you peer out the window of an aeroplane, your life (and all your worries) suddenly shrinks to insignificant proportions. In seat 44K, all there is to think about is the next movie you're going to watch and what sort of yummy surprises you might find wrapped up on the dinner tray. So right after Steph yelled at Dad and slammed the laundry door, I boarded my imaginary plane. And that's when the most incredible thing happened...

'Miss Hathaway,' the hostess said as she greeted me at the door. 'Lovely to see you again.'

'Hello, Tabitha,' I said, reading her nametag. 'Yes, it feels like ages since I've had a spell in 44K.'

'We were worried about you, Sunday. Thought you might be flying with *someone else.*'

'Not at all,' I said. 'I'm perfectly happy with *ThinAir.*'

'Well, have we got a surprise for you, Miss Hathaway. Do you know what it means to be *upgraded?*'

'Does that mean you get to skip a year at school?'

'No,' chuckled the hostess. 'Come with me and I'll show you.' She ushered me to the left, and immediately the seats were a little bigger and not so squashed in together.

'This is business class,' she said, leading me past rows and rows of seats. Then we came to a curtain that was buttoned down on one side. She swept it open, ushered me in and quickly closed it again behind us. 'Now, Sunday, because you're such a loyal customer, we've reserved a seat for you in our *first class* cabin. Seat 2A, Miss Hathaway, right up the very front of the plane.'

'Sunny?' Dad said, 'Did you hear what I said? I asked if you've seen Flora's beanie. I had it just a moment ago.'

'Found it!' I said coming back to reality. It was wedged down the side of the pram. I tried to slide it onto her head without her neck going all wobbly and without making her cry. Then Dad and I set off, and before we were even out of our street, Flora was asleep.

'Was I this much trouble?' I asked. 'Is that why you only had one of me?'

'Flora's no trouble,' said Dad. 'She's just a baby, doing what babies do. Steph's having a bit of a tired patch, that's all. She'll come good. But we might get Guff to move in for a while and lend a hand.'

'Cool!' I said, because Auntie Guff is my favourite auntie. (Come to think of it, Auntie Guff is my *only* auntie, so that makes having a favourite a whole lot more politically correct.) Auntie Guff knows absolutely everything there is to know about stuff that most people think is *flaky*. You know, like crystals and past lives and auras and chakras. She also works behind the scenes on TV shows and films, so I get to hear stories about actors and what sorts of diets they're on, and how some of them miss out on roles because they've had too much Botox and have lost their facial expressions.

I helped Dad make dinner so that Steph could rest, but Flora woke up grizzly and it took a long time for Steph to settle her back down again. There wasn't much anyone could do to help, 'cos most of the time all Flora wanted was Steph's boobs.

'Just start without me,' said Steph, with Flora almost

dozing over her shoulder. 'She's got a sixth sense for meal times. The minute the food's on the table ...'

'No no no,' said Dad. 'I want us all to have dinner together. She's almost there – look, she can hardly keep her eyes open. Want to try putting her down?'

Steph gently peeled Flora from her shoulder and laid her in the pram. Then she started rocking it. Flora's eyes shot open and her face winced up as though she was about to cry, but then she suddenly relaxed and drifted off to sleep. Dad wheeled the pram over to his seat, so that he could keep it rocking while we had dinner.

'I haven't even had time to have a shower today,' sighed Steph as she sat down. 'Anyhow, hardly very interesting. How's things in the outside world, Sunny? Are you all settled in at Carmelene's?'

'Pretty much. Although being there makes it impossible not to feel sad sometimes. And seriously, I seem to be the only one who misses Granny Carmelene because I'm the only one who really knew her. Recently, I mean. Willow's made herself a racetrack right around the house, and we're even thinking of starting up our own neighbourhood doggie entertainment business. It was kind of Lyall's idea, which is a major worry because he's going to think he's the boss and I can tell you right now ...'

I noticed a tear rolling down Steph's face, and she was biting into her bottom lip, trying to stop it from wobbling.

I felt awful. It must have been something I said that made her so upset, but I couldn't think what. I mean, I thought Steph *liked* dogs. I looked over to Dad, hoping he could do something to fix it, because, let's face it, Steph is kind of more his project than anyone else's.

'Sorry, Sunny, it's not you…it's just…*everything*,' Steph said, pushing her food around her plate. 'I'll be right. Just never imagined life could whittle down to wanting a night's sleep more than winning the lottery.'

'Have your dinner, love,' said Dad, still rocking Flora in the pram. 'And a nice bath. Sunny and I will take care of everything out here, won't we, Sunny?'

'Sure will,' I said, hoping like anything that Steph wouldn't break out into a full-blown blub. That'd mean seeing two adults cry in the same day. Don't they know that kids simply can't handle seeing them cry? They're *meant* to be setting an example. So, just in case, I was out of there. Especially as I'd been upgraded to first class.

'Have you had a chance to peruse the menu, Miss Hathaway?' the hostess said.

'Not yet,' I said. 'I'm still looking at all the in-flight movies.'

11.

Because it was holidays, I stayed at Dad and Steph's till halfway through Monday. I didn't sleep too well, though, because I could hear Steph up with Flora in the night, and at one stage Steph even had the TV on, which is right outside my bedroom door. I think she'd just plain forgotten I was there. Then, right when I was deeply asleep, Dad came in to say goodbye and woke me up *again*.

'Sorry, Sunny,' he said, 'but I won't see you all week. You be a big help to Steph today, now won't you?'

'Sure, Dad,' I said propping myself up on my elbows to give him a sleepy kiss goodbye. 'I'll try.'

But the problem was, I didn't really know *how* to be a big help to Steph. I wasn't even sure that she wanted me there, or *what* she wanted any more, for that matter.

I wasn't even sure that she wanted Flora. Still, I got up straight away, thinking I could offer to make some toast, and a cup of tea. I was good at that.

Steph was setting the baby bath up on the kitchen bench. 'Morning, Sunny,' she said. 'Want to help me bath Flora?'

'Sure,' I said, looking about to see where Flora actually was.

'She's in our bed. You can go get her if you like.'

Flora was awake, looking at a flickering shaft of light that was shifting about as the curtain waved. She looked so tiny all by herself in Dad and Steph's big bed.

'Hey Flora Galora!' I whispered, making sure I didn't give her a fright. Flora looked over to me, gave a huge gummy smile and kicked one leg frantically, as though it didn't actually belong to her body. 'Hello, Button, it's bath time.'

Flora kicked both legs and flapped her arms. It was a definite advantage in communicating with babies that I was already so good at communicating with dogs. Plus, I'd not only done a lot of research into Reverse Psychology, but also a lot of research into babies. I slid my arms gently underneath her, making sure I had her head well-supported, because babies' necks take a while to strengthen up. I rested her carefully over one shoulder. She smelt a little sour-milky and I noticed a wet patch on the sheets where she had been lying.

'It's a good thing you're having a bath, Flora,' I said, on my way out to the kitchen. 'Can I make you some toast, Steph?' I asked, handing Flora over. 'Maybe a cup of tea?'

'Oh dear, she's wet through,' said Steph, lying Flora on a towel and peeling off her sleep suit.

Steph didn't answer me, so I thought I'd just go ahead and make tea anyway. While Steph was bathing Flora I toasted and buttered some fruit bread too. Soon Flora was all swaddled up in a big fluffy towel.

'If you hold her for me, Sunny, I can get a load of washing on and change our bed.' She passed Flora over as though Flora was a bag of shopping, and didn't even notice the toast. Flora looked slightly bewildered.

'It's okay, Flora, it's just me again.'

'She'll be squawking for another feed soon,' said Steph, turning her back. There was something about the way Steph handled Flora that gave me mild throat ache. It was as if Flora was a big chore, rather than a cherished little person. I don't know what Steph was expecting when she wanted to have a baby, but she sure made it seem obvious that Flora wasn't 'it'.

I tried to be a *big help* to Steph as much as I could, but once she and Flora had both fallen asleep on the couch there wasn't much else I could think of to do. The dishwasher was empty, the kitchen was clean and the washing all done, so I called Dad and he said to leave a note to Steph and catch the bus back to Mum's before it got too peak-hourish. I slipped quietly out the back door, feeling a whole lot lighter just being out of Dad and Steph's house.

Being on the bus made me think of Finn and his stripy scarf again, and how he surely must have finished it because he probably wasn't allowed to watch TV, and how I didn't even know if he had brothers and sisters. I thought about Finn the whole way home, which I kind of found disturbing because my brain seemed to be on *autopilot*. It just seemed to want to wonder about the world of Finn, and notice how I liked all kinds of things about him, like the clothes he wore and how they weren't the sort of clothes that made him look like he was wearing a uniform like everyone else.

I could see Willow's snout squashed under our gate when I walked towards the house. She must have smelt me coming. At least I hoped she had, because I sure wouldn't like to think she'd spent the whole day with her nose squished under the gate like that – it was undignified.

'Willow!' I said as I opened the gate. 'Hello, girl. I'm home, and it's holidays!' She was crouching down on her back legs like a wind-up toy, ready to spring into action. I could tell she was trying her best not to jump up on me because ever since Mum went feral at her for tearing her favourite silk-velvet stockings, Willow's been clawing at people's legs far less. 'Come on, girl!' I said, dropping my backpack near the gate. 'I'll race you!'

Willow sprung off like a kangaroo, because if there's one thing that greyhounds are extra good at, it's acceleration. She had me outrun in milliseconds, did one super speedy racehorse lap of the house (checking behind her the whole way to make sure I was still in the race), and then broke into the Washing Machine, whirling around and around on the spot, which was a clear indication that her dog-joy levels were so high they literally sent her into a spin. There is nothing that makes Willow happier than when I do the Washing Machine too. I had a quick look around to make sure there was nobody about, because even though *They* say you should love like you've never been hurt before, and dance like nobody is watching, I'm still embarrassed even thinking about the older kids who saw me doing the Washing Machine with Willow at Elwood beach. Especially as I thought I'd made absolutely sure I was alone. Who would have thought to check if there was anyone watching from boats?

Willow barked at me as if to say, *Come on, Sunny, we haven't done the Washing Machine for ages and what is the point of having all this room and all this green spongy lawn if we can't do the Washing Machine any old time we like?*

Willow and I were in the full swing (or spin) when

the front door opened and Mum appeared on the porch, seeing one of her clients out.

'Oh, Sunday, you're home,' Mum said. 'You look just like a whirling dervish.' And both she and the client had a little giggle at my expense.

I gave Mum *the eyebrow*. Nothing brings the Washing Machine to a clunking halt quite like discovering your mum and some possibly lactose-intolerant client are looking on. Even Willow looked embarrassed and pretended she had suddenly found something fascinating to sniff in the garden.

Afterwards in the kitchen, Mum handed me a letter while I was gulping down a glass of water. 'Lovely envelope,' she said.

It was from Finn. I could tell by the Steiner rainbow on the back.

'Aren't you going to open it?' she asked. 'Might be an invitation.'

'I'll check it out later,' I said, remembering my lesson in nonchalance from Reverse Psychology. Let's face it, the last person you want to have around when opening a letter from an official pre-crush, maybe actual crush, is your mum. I put the letter in the back pocket of my jeans.

'How's it going with Steph and the baby?' Mum asked.

'Flora is sooo cute,' I said. 'But Steph's a bit weirded out.'

'Well I hope you're being helpful when you're around there,' she said. 'And not leaving all your things all over the house.'

'Oh don't worry, Mum,' I said. I couldn't wait any longer to open Finn's letter. 'I'm a *big* help,' I called over my shoulder as I ran upstairs to the turret.

'Sunny, come back here!' shouted Mum. 'I need you to run an errand for me.'

'I'll be down in a minute!' I yelled back, knowing I only had a small window before the precookeds got home. I closed the turret door behind me, took the envelope out of my pocket, carefully unstuck the pointy part and unfolded the letter. Finn had drawn colours over the whole page and then written really neatly over the top. So I was super-impressed, even before I'd read what he had to say:

Dear Sunny Hathaway,

See, I told you I'd write.

I was hoping you could help me with my homing pigeon training. You see, it's time for their first expedition, and if they find their way home I plan to bring back the pigeon post. If it works, I'm going to call it Pmail. Maybe I could bring them over to your place and set them free? Any day is fine. You can write back and tell me when is good

Your new friend,

Finn Fletcher Lomax (NFFFL)

Weird! I thought to myself. But kind of cool. Could he be serious about the pigeon post though?

'Sunday!' Mum called from downstairs. I put the letter in my bedside drawer and went back down to the kitchen. Mum was looking through a Thai recipe book, which I must say worried me slightly. Last time Mum made a Thai curry she used so much chilli that even Carl couldn't stomach it. It was around the time when Mum was still acting all girly and Carl was still doing a lot of fake enthusiasm about her cooking.

'I'd like you to run an errand for Settimio. He needs a few things at the chemist.'

'Do I get paid?' I asked, looking over her shoulder. 'And why do I have to do it? What about Lyall and Saskia?'

'They can do it next time. Besides, they're not home yet.'

'So, do I?' I repeated.

'Do you what?' asked Mum.

'Get paid?'

'No, Sunny. It's called *helping*, and maybe one day, when you're an old lady, and unfortunate enough to have a broken leg and a broken nose, there might be people around to help you too.'

'What's for dinner?' I asked.

'Thai fish cakes,' Mum said, and she gave me a fifty-dollar note and a list of things to pick up for Settimio. 'And no junk food, Sunny.'

I took a deep breath as I approached Settimio's door. Surely he wouldn't close it in my face when he knew I had a parcel for him. I could hear him clunking about and there was a warm waft of garlic in the air and the sound of a radio. I knocked gently on the door. The radio faded out as if it had been switched off at the wall, and Settimio appeared in the doorway, leaning on one crutch. Obviously this time he'd been expecting me.

'Come!' he said, motioning with his head. 'Inside.'

The kitchen was hobbit-house small, with a round wooden table in the middle and a real wood stove with a fire inside. Off the kitchen was a door to the sitting room and I could see old Marmalade in there, safely asleep on a chair. I put the chemist parcel on the kitchen table.

'There you go, Settimio,' I said politely. 'Do you need help with anything else?' I was hoping like crazy he'd say no, so I could scoot off as soon as possible, but then I noticed the shoe box on the table. The one I'd seen through the telescope. Sitting on top was a heart-shaped locket on a silver chain. I was overcome with curiosity.

'That's nice,' I said, pointing to the locket.

Settimio looked at me suspiciously before picking it up and opening the tiny heart-shaped frame.

'Your grandmother was *good* woman,' he said, like an accusation. 'It belongs to her; I find it buried in the garden.

For many years now I have kept this locket.'

'Why?' I asked. 'If you found it, why didn't you give it back to her?' It was becoming glaringly obvious to me that not only was Settimio a dog-and-child-hater but clearly also a thief. My thoughts were interrupted by Settimio handing me the locket.

'Not lost.' He scolded. 'Carmelene, she throw away.' He flicked the air with one hand as though he was tossing confetti into a gusty wind. 'When your Grandfather Henry leave.'

I looked closely at the tiny photograph inside. It was Grandpa Henry all right. I recognised him from other photos I'd seen.

'He brok-ed her heart. She never trust again.'

'I know, double betrayal,' I said. 'It's the worst kind. Mum told me.'

Settimio took my two hands in his and closed all our hands around the locket.

'You have, Sunday. It is yours. Carmelene would like it to be in this manner.' He squeezed my hands together for a moment and gave them two solid shakes, as if he was sealing the deal and there were to be no arguments.

'Wow, thanks,' I said, gently releasing his grip and wondering why he was suddenly being so nice to me. It was dead confusing I can tell you.

But one thing I did understand was that Settimio

really missed Granny Carmelene, and that he'd known her for a lot longer than I had. I know it seems obvious, but I guess with him being so mean and all, I just hadn't been able to imagine him and Granny Carmelene being friends. He must have been having mountains of sad thoughts. Mountains. Maybe he needed Bruce and Terry?

I didn't tell Mum about the locket. I don't know why. I put it in my bedside table on top of Finn's letter. But beforehand, I looked at it more closely. It had a silver engraving of an angel on the outside of the heart. I remembered back to my secret trip to Tasmania with Granny Carmelene, and how she'd held my hand deep down in King Solomon's Cave. And how I'd seen an angel disappearing up and out of a crack in the ceiling towards the light.

I turned off my lamp and waited until my eyes adjusted to the dark. I could just make out the outline of the cypress trees by Settimio's cottage, and for the first time I felt comforted by the idea that he was living down there and wondered if Granny Carmelene had felt the same way. I was thankful that she had had Settimio to watch over her for all those years. And maybe, just maybe, it could be possible that if I liked Granny Carmelene and Granny Carmelene liked me, and Granny Carmelene liked Settimio, and Settimio liked her, then possibly, just possibly, one day Settimio and I might like one another too.

12.

I woke up the next morning thinking about Finn, which was slightly disturbing, because usually I woke up and simply thought about breakfast. So even though writing a letter kind of felt like homework, I conjured up my best handwriting and did it anyway.

Dear NFFFL,

Thanks for the letter. Luckily I still have some nice writing paper that my Grandmother gave me last Christmas. She's dead now. That's why we moved into her old house. Do you have siblings? I have two (precooked) but they're not here all the time because they are also victims of divorce and live in two houses, like me.

So anyway, you can come and visit and Mum said it's fine to bring the pigeons as long as they're in a box because we've got a dog and a very old cat.

It's pretty weird that you don't use a telephone. I don't think I know anyone who doesn't have a telephone actually.

Have you finished your scarf?

Come over next Monday at ten o'clock because I'm going to my Dad's at the weekend.

Bye then,

Your new friend Sunny Hathaway (NFSH)

It was a rainy old day so there was absolutely no point getting out of my pyjamas. I climbed downstairs and knocked on Lyall's door. We had planned to make the brochures for Boredom Control, and Saskia had convinced us that she'd be the best one to design them as she was almost certain she had a full-blown case of dyslexia. I had to make sure Lyall didn't sleep all morning.

'The brochures?' I said poking my head inside. I think I was trying to start acting like a manager type, just in case he really did think he owned the business. I heard him grunt and turn over, so I went and knocked on Saskia's door, across the hall. 'Saskia, you awake?'

'Come in,' she said. 'I've been working on ideas.' I pushed open the door. There were drawings laid out all over the floor.

'I did a lot of work in the night,' she said, snapping the lid back on one of her textas.

'Wow! They look amazing.' I picked up one drawing. It was a whole group of assorted dogs running around an obstacle course. 'Did you sleep at all?'

'Not really,' said Saskia. 'But a lot of artists work through the night. You just have to ride the wave of inspiration when it comes.' She did an enormous yawn, which made me yawn too, even though I'd just woken up.

'Maybe you'd better get some more sleep,' I said. 'Lyall's still snoozing too. Besides, all this yawning is contagious.'

'Maybe you're right,' she said, yawning some more and flopping back into bed.

I really wanted to slide down the banister, but I could hear Mum down in the library, so I took the stairs the regular old way instead.

'Morning, sweetheart,' she said, looking at her watch. 'I've got my first client in half an hour. I'm just making sure the library's ready for tonight's meeting.'

Mum and Carl had invited the neighbours over to see if they'd be interested in forming an environmental action group. It was Carl's idea, of course. Besides the fact that he made a living out of trying to get huge corporations to reduce their carbon footprint, Carl said it would be wrong to be living in such a super-privileged way, in such a ridiculously big house, without setting an example for other people living in super-privileged ways in ridiculously big houses. But it was completely obvious to me that what the neighbours were *mostly* interested in was having a stickybeak at our house.

'So, Sunny,' Mum went on. 'Will you three be mindful that I'm working today and not be too rowdy?'

'Sure, Mum,' I said. 'We're just making our brochures. It's not a very noisy activity.'

'And if there's a break in this weather, Willow will need a walk.'

'I've got to go post a letter, so I'll take Willow with me.'

'Make sure you call by Settimio's place and see if he needs anything at the shops.'

'Consider it done, Mum.'

But as Mum's string of clients came and went and Lyall and Saskia didn't wake up, and it was *still* raining, I snuck Willow onto the couch in the gameless games room and we watched hours of daytime television without anybody to tell us not to. It was just like old times, only in a bigger house.

That night Carl was stressed to the max, which pretty much meant that he and Lyall would end up having an argument. It's just the way it is with them, because when it comes to Lyall, Carl's got what you might call a *short fuse*.

'Now listen, Lyall,' said Carl, 'I don't want you goofing off on MySpace all night; do you hear? I want you to help serve refreshments.'

'Okay. Chill, Dad,' said Lyall.

'Don't *chill* me, Lyall. There are jobs to do. It's our first night and we've got three people coming, which isn't bad considering most punters around here think they need four-wheel drive trucks just to get their kids to school.'

'Oh no,' said Saskia, making up a jug of lemon cordial. 'Don't get Dad started on the *truck* issue.'

'They should be banned,' said Carl. 'Or, if you really need a truck to keep up with the Joneses, you should at least have to pay more to register the damn things. You wouldn't believe the scene the other day in Malvern Road. Trucks everywhere. All with just one person in them. It's a disgrace.'

'What do you suggest then, Carl, shared Kombi Vans run on bio-diesel?' I said.

'Sunny!' said Mum, giving me *the eyebrow*. 'Don't be smart.'

'What I *am* suggesting Sunny, is *change*. Is that such a difficult concept?'

Apart from the fact that change *was* a difficult concept for me, I didn't like it when Carl told me off, because he isn't actually my father. When Dad tells me off I don't even care, but Carl made my cheeks burn red. I wished I could turn invisible. To be honest, I think Mum should have stuck up for me. It's not as if he doesn't have two kids of his own to vent on.

'Lyall,' continued Carl. 'I'll need you to get the whiteboard out of the laundry for me. And Saskia, once you've finished making the cordial you can put out a plate of biscuits too. And some glasses, of course.'

'Sure, Dad,' said Saskia, who knew the exact level of agreeability to prevent an argument when Carl was stressed.

'Sunny, it can be your job to clear up afterwards.'

'Fine,' I said.

'*Lyall!*' Carl yelled. 'How many times do I have to ask you to go and get the whiteboard?'

'Come on, Lyall,' I said, wanting an excuse to leave the room. 'I'll help.'

Once the three guests arrived, and Mum and Carl were occupied in the library, Lyall and Saskia and I went up to Lyall's room and finished our brochures for Boredom Control. All we had to do was print some off and we'd be ready to deliver in the morning.

After the meeting, Carl came upstairs to let us know the guests had gone, which was my cue to start the clearing up. Thankfully, he seemed a little more relaxed.

'These are excellent,' he said, looking at our brochures.

'Saskia did them,' I said.

'Dad,' said Saskia. 'Sometimes when I'm reading, the words swirl around on the page and the letters get all mixed up.'

'She's lying, Dad,' said Lyall. 'She's just trying to convince you she's dyslexic.'

'Go away, Lyall. Dad, it's true. I told Mrs Pattison but she just ignored me.'

'Did she, darl?' said Carl, putting the brochures down. 'Oh well, you kids better get ready for bed.'

'Dad, did you even listen to me?' whined Saskia.

That was when I went downstairs to the library. I grabbed a dishcloth from the kitchen sink, wheeled the trolley into the library and parked it by the door. I was humming a tune, because sometimes tunes come into my head. I might never have heard the tune before, but I hum along. I took all the glasses off the old oval table and remembered how Granny Carmelene had first shown me her old maps there, next to a big vase of hydrangeas. I wiped down the table and checked around for anything else that needed to go back to the kitchen.

I was stacking and checking and wiping and humming

away when *the most* freaky thing happened, and if I tell you about it you're not allowed to think I'm a nut-job, okay?

I heard soft clear music coming from somewhere up high. At first I thought there must be speakers that I hadn't noticed before, but I looked all around and couldn't find any. Then the music got louder, as if someone had turned the volume up and my skin went all tingly. It seemed to be coming from the ceiling near the wooden ladder used for the out-of-reach books. I stood at the lowest step and looked up.

And that's when I saw it. An angel! Just like the one I'd seen with Granny in King Solomon's Cave. I swear on my life it's true. It was an angel I tell you. Halo, wings and all.

I didn't tell Mum and Carl about what I'd seen, because let's face it, if they don't believe in Father Christmas or the Easter Bunny, they were hardly going to believe I'd seen an angel (for the second time) were they? Besides, I kind of wanted to keep it to myself because it was so lovely and special and just for me – like Finn, and Granny Carmelene's locket. Arguing about it was going to make it all muddy and torn and belong to everyone else.

That night I snuck Willow into the turret to sleep at the end of my bed, because if the angel visited me again, I wanted to share it with someone who wouldn't have any trouble believing.

13.

When I woke up the next morning I wasn't thinking about breakfast and I wasn't thinking about Finn. I was thinking about angels and how maybe, just maybe, I might have imagined the whole thing – twice. And how if that was the case then maybe, just maybe, I *was* a nut-job.

But then I started thinking about how angels are well-known as messengers and guardians, so maybe, just maybe, the angel in the library *was* real and had something to do with Granny Carmelene. Could she be trying to communicate from the *other side*, like from *nowhere*? One things was for sure, I had to tell someone, even if it was just to reassure myself that I wasn't going crazy. But would I tell Lyall and Saskia and risk them making fun of me for ever, or would I tell Mum and Carl and suffer the inevitable frustration of them not believing me at all? I couldn't tell Claud because she was away. And Finn? Well, I kind of wanted Finn to like me, I f you know what I mean.

So I spent the next half-hour constructing a handy flow chart, which can often help if you're having trouble knowing the best path to take. Perhaps just check at the end of the book in case I remembered to include it.

After studying the chart and weighing up my options, I decided to barge on in and tell Lyall and Saskia.

'It's true! It was an angel in the library. I was thinking about Granny Carmelene and then there it was!'

The three of us were up in Lyall's room, printing the Boredom Control brochures.

Lyall burst out laughing. 'Yeah right, Sunny. You tricked me once, you're not going to suck me in with angels too. How many brochures do you think we should print? About fifty? We'll also need some to stick onto street poles.'

Maybe Lyall's response served me right. At least he didn't say *I* was bats.

'You *should* believe in angels, Lyall, the Catholics practically invented them,' I said.

'*I* believe in angels!' Saskia said. 'And Sunny's right, Lyall. You should believe in them because they're in the Bible.'

'Exactly,' I said. 'And I *know* they're real, because now

I've seen one twice. I attract them. It's obvious.'

'That's hardly proof, Sunny,' said Lyall. 'I'd need to see it for myself, or at least have solid evidence. I mean, why didn't you take a photo, Sunny?'

'Well, Lyall, I guess that would be because I didn't happen to have a camera with me. Der.'

All of a sudden Saskia became terribly excited. 'I know!' she squealed. 'We can catch the angel with your surveillance equipment, Lyall, just like how at Mum's we—'

'Shoosh, Saskia!' scolded Lyall, punching her in the arm. 'You breathe one word of that and I'll seriously put your head down the insinkerator.'

I gave Lyall *the eyebrow*, as if to say, *Surveillance huh? Sounds completely dodgy.* But then I thought, *who am I to talk? I spy on an old man through a telescope.*

Carl appeared at the door. 'I'm off to work now, guys,' he said. 'What have you got planned for the day?'

'Sunny saw an angel, Dad,' Saskia said.

'That's great, sweetheart,' Carl said, kissing Saskia goodbye.

'I did, Carl, actually I saw one twice,' I said.

'Wonderful, Sunny. Now, you kids get some fresh air today. There's no sign of rain. You were inside all day yesterday.'

'We'll be delivering our brochures,' said Lyall.

'Excellent, oh and that reminds me, can you grab a stack

of flyers for the action group and deliver them as well?'

'Sure,' we all said at once.

We tried to save on brochures by targeting houses with obvious signs of dog ownership. Having Willow with us made it easy because whenever we passed a house with a resident dog, the smell of Willow made the other dog rush to the fence barking.

'I really do think there are a lot of bored dogs around here,' Saskia said, rolling up a brochure and sliding it into a letterbox. Boredom Control could really take off.'

'It's a pity that Buster lives so far away – he's convinced you can teach dogs to meditate and says he's had success on more than one occasion,' I said.

'Well,' said Saskia, 'I believe it. If you can hypnotise a chicken—'

'You believe anything, Saskia,' said Lyall.

'Do not, Lyall.'

'Come on, you guys, do you have to argue about absolutely everything?' I said.

'Exactly, Sunny,' said Lyall. 'That's why scientists invented proof. So there'd be nothing left to argue about, and that's why, as soon as we get home, I'm going to hook up my surveillance system in the library. If there really is an angel, Sunny, we'll catch it on the monitor.'

14.

It was the weekend, which usually meant bacon and eggs, but Mum was having all sorts of trouble with her poaching, and we didn't even have any bacon.

'Blast!' Mum said, as she scooped a lonely yolk out of the poaching pot.

'Did you give it a dash of vinegar, love?' asked Carl, pouring coffee.

'Yes,' said Mum. 'Vinegar and a pinch of salt. Maybe the eggs are old?'

'Dad, can I have a coffee too?' asked Lyall.

'No, Lyall,' said Carl.

'Can I?' asked Saskia.

'No, Saskia. Coffee isn't for children.'

'Here, Sunny,' said Mum, handing me a side plate with

the little yellow ball of poached yolk. 'May as well give this to Willow. I might give up on poached eggs and we'll have scrambled instead?'

'And bacon?' I asked hopefully.

Mum gave Carl *the eyebrow*, as if to say, *I'm having enough trouble with these eggs, you tell the children how we've decided to ruin their lives by putting a ban on deliciously crispy bacon.*

'Well, said Carl. 'Alex and I have decided to ruin your lives by putting a ban on deliciously crispy bacon.'

'Daaaaad-uh!' yelled Lyall and Saskia in chorus, but due to Carl not being my dad and all, I couldn't join in. I just gave him *the eyebrow* as if to say, *Nice one, Carl – let me guess, you're going to try to convince us that tofu can taste just as good as bacon.*

'Come on, you guys, be a little open-minded. Besides, you can get some amazing tofu products now that taste *just like bacon*. You won't even know the difference.'

I wasn't in the mood for arguing about bacon. We had three appointments to think about, with potential customers who had responded to our brochure. That meant a lot of smooth-talking and good manners, which you have to admit is sometimes an exhausting combination. Especially for an introvert. Hopefully by the end of it we'd have our very first clients for Boredom Control.

A woman called Kara Bleakly was on the top of our list. She lived in Foster Street. In Carmichael Drive we were to visit a guy called Ritchie Draper followed by a family called the Archers down in Howard Crescent.

'Now, kids,' said Carl, stacking the dishwasher as we were ready to leave. 'Make sure you remember to invite all three of them to our next meeting.'

'Yes,' said Mum, 'and tell them about how we're turning our land into a community vegetable plot.'

'What about farming some organic pigs?' I suggested, but everyone just stared at me straight-faced.

'Don't be silly, Sunny,' said Mum. 'You cried all the way through *Babe*.'

If you ask me, everything about Kara Bleakly's house was bleak. For a start it was all the one bleak colour, kind of grey stone with dried out slats of wood and a jutting-out box of cold empty glass. I think it's what *They* call *Modern*. There was a high stone fence across the front with a locked gate and an intercom button. Right when Saskia buzzed, a black snout appeared under the gate, accompanied by some rather loud snorting. Then the gate opened and we were greeted by Kara Bleakly, who looked as bleak as her name and her house suggested. Even her voice was bleak and all on one level like the low hum of a fridge. I think *They* call it monotone. The only thing connected to Kara Bleakly that *wasn't* bleak was her big fat black bounding labrador, Sophia.

'You must be Lyall,' Kara said, holding out her hand.

'Yeah, hi, and this is my sister Saskia and this is my – um – kind of like stepsister, kind of like—'

'I'm Sunny,' I said holding out my hand. 'As in Sunday.'

Kara Bleakly had one of those limp, wet-fish handshakes, but I didn't have to endure it for too long because Sophia jumped up and almost knocked me over.

'Down, Sophia,' said Kara. 'Sorry, you can see she's got a lot of energy – most of which she puts towards digging holes, I'm afraid. Oh and over-eating, of course.' Kara nodded at all the holes Sophia had dug in the garden, and that's when she noticed Saskia's shoes.

'Oh dear, you're wearing those unfortunate shoes. What are they called again? Crocs?'

Saskia blushed with embarrassment as we all looked down at her red socks and purple Crocs. There was an awful silence that seemed to last forever, until she said (in a tiny little Miss Mousy voice), 'They're actually *really* comfortable.'

'I'm sorry, Saskia, that came out all wrong. They're a perfect shoe for a child, it's the adults who wear them I worry about. They really have taken over like the plague. Everywhere you look it's Crocs, Crocs, Crocs. All year round. Why anyone would want to wear buckets on their feet is beyond me. They really do look ridiculous.'

'How old is Sophia?' I asked, trying to change the subject, but it didn't really work because Kara Bleakly kept on and on about Crocs, and then she bent down to our level and leant in like she was about to tell us a big secret, and before we knew it we were all in a huddle in Kara Bleakly's bleak front garden, and she whispered, 'Guess what?'

And we whispered back, 'What?'

'I wouldn't date a man who wore Crocs if he were the last male specimen on this earth.'

For me, that was solid proof that Kara Bleakly didn't have the first idea about what to say to children. You know, like those adults who have nothing to say to you other than *How's school?*

'So,' said Kara. 'I'm working ridiculously long hours at the moment.' Then she leant down once more and started talking in a hushed voice again, like she had *the* most incredible thing to say. We all leant in close, only to hear that all Kara Bleakly wanted to tell us was: 'Whatever you do, don't become a lawyer.'

'I want to be an artist,' said Saskia. 'I'm even—'

'Do you think you could manage Sophia for an hour a day?' Kara asked. 'I'll give you a key to the gate and you can get her any time that suits.'

'Sure,' said Lyall.

The Archers had an Australian cattle dog (which Mum says is the wrong sort of dog to have in the city), a red heeler called Banjo.

'He could run all day and it still wouldn't be enough,' said Mr Archer. 'And we just don't have the time any more, not since the twins came along.'

'Does Banjo like to chase balls?' I asked, thinking it might be a good way of wearing him out.

'Sure does,' said Mr Archer. 'But he mostly likes to chase ankles.'

'Oh,' I said, wondering how exactly that might pan out.

'Can he swim?' asked Lyall.

'Because we've got our own patch of river,' said Saskia. 'With a bend in it.'

'Sounds like you've got it all worked out down there at Boredom Control headquarters,' said Mr Archer. 'How 'bout you take him for three sessions each week?'

'Perfect,' I said, shaking Mr Archer's hand.

Next was Woolfie. He was an enormous shaggy Irish wolfhound belonging to Ritchie Draper, who was the first person we remembered to talk to about Mum and Carl's sustainability group. He looked like a bit of a greenie, even if he did have a job thinking up ads for a living, which Carl says is a profession that abuses its power to manipulate the masses.

'Mmm, sustainability action group, huh? Sounds like a top idea,' said Ritchie. 'You can count me in.'

Ritchie also signed Woolfie up for three sessions a week at Boredom Control.

'Wow, with all three dogs that's one hundred and ten dollars a week!' said Lyall on the way home. 'And I really like Ritchie; he seems cool.'

'Lyall, we used to make more than that in just one day selling pizzas, remember?' I said. 'Our record night was one hundred and fifty dollars! Now we have to work *every day*, well with Sophia at least, and three days a week with the others, and all for less money.'

'How much do we get each?' asked Saskia.

Lyall took out his phone to use the calculator part.

'It's thirty-six dollars point six six six six six six seven cents, and I don't care, Sunny – it's not always about money.'

'No,' I said sarcastically. 'Business isn't about money; how could I be so silly?'

'Advertising would be such a cool job,' Lyall said, to avoid the harsh reality that pizzas made better business sense than dogs.

'Did anyone notice what I noticed?' I asked. 'Ritchie's not as cool as you might think, Lyall.'

'Why?'

'I saw a pair of Crocs. Bright tragic green ones, right there on Ritchie's front verandah.

15.

Auntie Guff was over at Dad and Steph's when I got there. She was cooking up a storm, as Dad would say, making loads of freezer meals for later. The whole house was steamed up with the smell of lamb-shank soup.

'Sunny! Long time no see, Miss!' Guff held her arms out wide and I gave her a hug, which always makes me want to sneeze on account of Guff's frizzy hair that tickles your nose. Maybe it's the frizz that's stopping Guff from finding a boyfriend? I mean, it'd have to be an issue, wouldn't it: a girlfriend with hair that made you sneeze?

'Hi, Guff!' I said, pulling back a little. 'How long are you staying?'

'It's all a bit up in the air right now. I'm waiting for the go-ahead on a film shoot in South Africa. You know how it goes, Sunny. They'll probably call me in a panic the day before and I'll have to drop everything and fly on over.'

Dad came out of the bedroom, closing the door quietly behind him.

'Still both asleep,' he said in a hushed voice, but right when he said so Flora started crying. 'Whoops, spoke too soon,' he said, rolling his eyes.

A few minutes later Steph came out from the bedroom all bleary eyed (without Flora), and walked across the lounge room to the kitchen.

'Oh, hi, Sunny,' she said, rubbing her eyes, and kind of pushing past me to get to the sink. Flora was still crying from her cot in Dad and Steph's room, but Steph was acting as if she hadn't even noticed.

'Shall I go pick her up?' I asked, because apart from the sound of Flora crying being one of the most unbearable sounds on earth, I was absolutely dying to see her.

'What? Oh, I guess so,' said Steph blankly.

Flora stopped crying the moment I picked her up. I'm sure she remembered who I was, because babies (like dogs) have far better memories than people give them credit for. But she soon started squirming and grouching again, turning her little open birdie mouth towards me as though perhaps she thought I might feed her. I put the end of my little finger in her mouth because I've seen Dad do that and it can really help. Flora sucked it for a moment, but it didn't work for long. She a good look at me, realised for certain that I wasn't Steph, arched her back and shifted her crying into second gear. I carried her over to Steph, who was on the couch flicking through channels on the TV.

'I think she's hungry,' I said, getting ready to hand Flora over.

Steph sighed and heaved herself up as if she actually *resented* being the only one Flora really needed. She pulled a cushion in behind her and stacked some around her, including one for her lap. Then, without even looking up from the TV, she pulled up her shirt, undid her bra, reached out for Flora and plonked her on her breast.

As I watched I sure hoped that breast milk didn't transmit emotions because Steph really had become one big moody-broody person in a permanent grump. With everyone. But the scariest part was the way Steph hardly seemed to *look* at Flora, or smile at her. I could feel in my intuition that this was just plain wrong, not to mention rude. I mean, I felt unwelcome and I'm old enough to kind of know it's just because Steph isn't getting much sleep. How's Flora meant to work it out? It's not as if Flora has any imaginary inventions to help her out when life becomes overwhelming, like a seat up in the sky where they treat you even better than before because you've been all upgraded...

They give you pyjamas in first class. And a whole package full of skin products, as well as those eye-mask things and a pair of socks. I put my pyjamas on straight away, even though it was still daytime. I felt instantly comforted about Steph, confident, even, that she'd snap out of her bad mood and realise how lucky she was to have her very own baby Flora.

The hostess appeared with a tray of steaming hot refresher towels piled up in scrolls. She noticed my clothing in a pile on the floor.

'Would you like me to hang those up for you, Miss Hathaway?' she said, handing me a towel with a pair of tongs.

'Thank you,' I said, tossing the hot towel from one hand to the other until it was cool enough to put over my face. Then I used it to clean both my hands.

The hostess held out a small plastic tray for me to dispose of the crumpled face washer.

'Thanks so much,' I said, and reached for the menu, feeling very excited about the upgrade. And that's when it all went horribly wrong.

It was the food, I tell you. There was hardly *anything* that I liked. It was all so horribly … *adult*. It was an absolute and undeniable disaster!

See for yourself:

Tartlet of mushroom ragout with porcini
Yuck.

Chilled cauliflower soup with salmon roe
Cold Cauliflower! As if hot cauliflower isn't bad enough – but with fish eggs? Please!

Leek and Roquefort soup with chervil
I've been craving those particular three ingredients. Not.

Prawn and celeriac remoulade
Maybe, if I was absolutely desperate I could eat the prawn part.

Signature steak sandwich with relish
Now we're talking, depending on whose signature you get.

They'd even ruined the desserts:

Ginger cake
Ginger! Why not chocolate or banana?

Raspberry friand
At least it's not a ginger friend.

Gypsy cream biscuits
Are they stolen?

Fresh whole fruit
As if I don't have enough of that from Mum.

Chocolate coated vanilla ice-cream
Why didn't you say so earlier?!!

I buzzed the hostess and ordered two serves of ice-cream.

'That won't be long, Sunday,' she said.

'Can I ask you just one more thing?'

'Certainly,' she said. 'Anything at all.'

'Any chance I could have my old seat back? No offence, but I was kind of fond of seat 44K.'

'Sunny! Hel*lo*!' said Auntie Guff, waving her hands across my eyes. 'Anyone home? You're miles away.'

'I was,' I said. 'Sorry, I think I'm in need of a snack.'

'How about some soup,' asked Guff. 'And I picked up some fresh bread too.' She nodded towards a brown parcel on the bench, all wrapped up like a present.

'And a cup of tea?' said Dad, looking up from the paper. 'Be a love, Sunny, and put the kettle on, would you? We'll make a pot.'

I filled the kettle at the tap while remembering I'd been saving up my angel questions for Guff. 'That reminds me, Guff,' I said. 'I've been meaning to ask – do you think angels are a way dead people communicate with the people left behind?'

Guff looked a little shocked. I guess she'd just been thinking about soup all afternoon.

'Lordy, Sunny! I presume you're talking about your grandmother?' she said, passing me a bowl of steaming-hot soup. 'You must miss her, huh?' She unwrapped the bread and cut me off a big fresh slice. 'Butter?'

'Yes please. Do you believe in angels, Guff?' I asked. 'I mean, it's fine not to, it's just that I saw one the other day, and I thought maybe it was Granny Carmelene trying to give me a message or something.'

Guff shot Dad an anxious look as he peered up momentarily from the paper. It was as if each was hoping the other one would come up with the answer. I dipped my bread in the soup and took a bite.

'Mmm, delicious,' I said.

Dad had suddenly busied himself making tea, probably so that he didn't have to get involved in a conversation about spirits and angels. Then he started humming to himself, which is Dad's version of having a *Do Not Disturb* sign on his forehead. He also made extra loud clunking noises with the crockery.

'Sorry, Guff,' I said. 'It's just that you've got those angel cards and all. I thought you might have inside information.'

'Gosh, okay, um, I have heard of angel-sightings, Sunny, but I've not actually seen one myself.'

'Do you think it's possible to see an angel on a surveillance monitor? I mean, you know how vampires don't show up in mirrors or on film? Is it the same with angels do you think?'

'I honestly couldn't tell you, Sunny,' said Guff.

'Guff?' I said, sensing it might be time to change the topic.

'Yep.'

'Why is your name Guff?'

'Hasn't your dad told you?' she said, chuckling (probably with relief). Even Dad stopped humming and clunking. 'Like many nicknames it came about because when I was small I couldn't say my name properly.'

'How do you get Guff out of Justine?'

'I used to say Guffgeen, apparently. I don't know, I was probably only two years old at the time, but the Guff part stuck.'

'Do they call you Guff at work?'

'Yep.'

'What about if you went on a date, would you say, *Hi, I'm Guff*?'

'Well maybe not if it was a complete stranger. What's with all the questions, Sunny?'

'Nothing really, just wondering.'

'Is it sad not having your grandmother around?'

Dad started humming again as he got the milk out of the fridge.

'It is lately,' I said. 'But luckily I managed to get my hands on some Woe-Be-Gone grief repellent. Bruce and Terry put me onto it.'

'Who the hell are Bruce and Terry?' Dad asked.

'They're grief bouncers. They stop sad thoughts getting in. I mean, it's not exactly easy moving into a house that someone just died in. Anyway, Bruce and Terry have been great, but now I'm thinking that Granny Carmelene might actually be still around. You know, in the form of an angel. We're trying to prove it by catching the angel on Lyall's surveillance camera. I've also got a new friend called Finn, who knits and who no one's even met. He's coming around on Monday with a box full of pigeons.'

'Ah ha,' said Guff looking bewildered.

'That explains everything,' said Dad, heading back to the paper.

'I kind of have to replace Claud, you dig?'

'Replace?'

'Since Buster came along, I've lost my one-on-one friend, and, well, I need a new best friend. It's really clear.'

'Of course.'

'Have you been dating much yourself, Guff?'

'I've given up, Sunny. Most dates I've been on lately

have bored me to tears, and I'm not really sold on this one-on-one thing, Sunny. It's like the whole world is only set up for couples and families. What happens to the people who aren't part of a couple-centric ideal?' Guff suddenly looked puffed up and angry. 'And I'm just not buying into it, to be perfectly frank, Sunny'

'Frank? Who's Frank?' I asked.

'Sunny Hathaway, you are *incorrigible*!' said Guff.

Later on, I typed 'angel sightings' into YouTube. There were heaps of clips, but to be frank (which Guff had told me actually means *straightforward* and *to the point*), I couldn't actually *see* an angel in any of them. Most of what were meant to be angels were just blurry marks that could have been something on the camera lens, like fluff, or a spider. In one clip there were just tiny white dots, and no matter how many different ways I looked at them I couldn't see an angel, just tiny white dots.

My angel was an angel of the traditional variety, with fluttery wings and a halo of golden light. So I googled for more info, but there was mostly stuff about guardian angels and how we're all meant to have been born with seven of them. I couldn't find a thing about angels that might be your grandmother or acting on your grandmother's behalf. Nothing at all.

Still, it wasn't that I needed proof or anything. I'm no

sceptic like Lyall. I believe all sorts of stuff without needing solid evidence. Because when I know something is true, it's not just a knowing I get in my head, but a knowing I get with my entire body.

16.

Dad dropped me back at Windermere on his way to work on Monday morning. I was dead excited because Finn was coming over at ten o'clock.

'Getting a bit of work done?' said Dad, nodding at the two vans from Green Plumbing parked in the driveway.

'We're getting rainwater tanks put in, and a grey water system for the garden, and solar hot water as well as solar everything else.'

'All very environmental of you,' said Dad.

'It's Carl,' I said. 'He says sustainability is everyone's responsibility.'

'Mmm,' said Dad. 'He's probably right.' He gave me a kiss on the cheek. 'I'll see you on Thursday. Can you make your own way over?'

'Sure,' I said, stepping out of the car. 'But Dad, does Steph actually *mind* me coming?' I asked.

'Course not! Besides, it's not up to Steph, it's up to me. See you Thursday.'

If you ask me, the way Dad answered me sounded pretty much like Steph *did* mind me being there. If Steph *really* didn't mind surely Dad would have put up much more of a fight to try to convince me otherwise. The thing is, I was starting to mind *Steph* being there. With her moods lately, I'd started wishing it could just be me, Dad and Flora.

Willow came running as soon as she heard the gate click open and threw herself at my feet and squirmed around on her back. I leant down and gave her some friendly dog-slaps on her big pokey-out greyhound chest.

'Oh, Willow, you're seriously *not* normal!' I said. Then she flipped back onto her legs in one movement and raced me to the front door, managing to cram in two laps of the rose garden and a few quick Washing Machines on her way.

'Hel-lo!' I yelled out as I opened the door. I could hear noises in the kitchen and could smell toast and coffee.

'Hi, sweetheart!' said Mum appearing in the entrance hall. She gave me a big hug and a kiss. 'I'm glad you're back. How's your little sister?'

'Mum, were you all grumpy with me when I was a baby? Like, when I cried or was hungry, was it a giant hassle?'

'Sunday! Of course not. Sleep deprivation is no fun, though. It's a form of torture. Have you had brekkie?'

'Yep,' I said. 'Mum, I seriously think Steph doesn't want me there. Maybe Dad only has me over because he has to.'

'I'm sure that's not true, love. She's probably just—'

'And most of all I'm worried for Flora because Steph never smiles at her or makes goo-goo noises, or even hardly *looks* at her, and it just makes me feel so empty and sad, and I'm sure Flora feels it too, and you're not meant to feel empty and sad when you're a baby, Mum. You're meant to feel like absolutely everything is all right.' My voice got a little quivery and I got a big case of throat ache.

'Oh, Sunny,' said Mum giving me a hug which made everything all the more quivery and achy. 'I'm sorry it's such a difficult time, darling.' She swept my hair back behind my ears. 'I know you love Flora, but you really mustn't feel so responsible for her. You'll worry yourself sick. Flora will be all right. You'll see.'

'Why don't you go and look out back?' said Mum. 'Lyall and Saskia worked all afternoon yesterday on an obstacle course for your dog business.'

I looked at my watch. I had two hours before Finn came over, presuming he was an on-time person. At least by then I wouldn't look so weepy. Let's face it, you really should hold back from crying in front of extremely new new best friends.

I stood on the back steps and blew my nose into a tissue. There were tradesmen everywhere, including all over the roof. Windermere was a construction zone. Carl had pegged out a whole area of lawn at the side of the vegetable garden, that I guessed was destined to become the community plots. I noticed Settimio leaning against his picket fence. He looked bewildered, as if maybe he thought the whole house was about to get bulldozed. I waved to him but he didn't wave back. It could have been that he had bad eyesight. Maybe that's how he got himself all banged up.

There was a flat area of lawn at the edge of the garden, right before it sloped down to the river bank. That's where Lyall and Saskia had set up their obstacle course, if *course* was the right word for what seemed to me to be a mess of strings, sticks and balls among a few witches hats.

I had to fight back a pang of jealousy that I wasn't a part of making it, but mostly I just wondered where the witches hats had come from. I had a strong feeling in my intuition that Lyall would have stolen them, for sure. That's exactly the sort of thing Lyall does. *Boy*, I thought to myself, *I go away for two days and the whole house is turned upside down!*

At exactly ten o'clock the doorbell rang. I was up in my room neatening things up a little. I couldn't find my favourite stripy hoodie anywhere and finally gave up looking for it when I remembered I must have left it at Dad's. I grabbed my second favourite non-stripy hoodie instead. I was glad Finn was an on-time person, like me. Seriously, I don't know why most people bother having a watch, other than to tell them how late they're running. Especially Dad and Claud.

Willow ran to the door with me, but I had to shut her in the library until I'd sussed out the pigeon situation. She gave me a look as if to say, *Well, all right, Sunny, but if I'm in here for too long I'll pee and I can't guarantee it won't be on the rug.*

'Oh, Willow,' I said gently closing the library door. 'Please don't.'

I took a deep breath and opened the front door. Finn was standing there in a navy-blue pinstriped suit jacket, strange jeans and his new stripy scarf. He was holding a flat crate with a wooden lid.

'Sunny Hathaway,' he said. 'Nice pad! You rich or something?'

'No, my grandma was – I think – don't know really. We kind of just got given the place.'

There was a sudden loud banging from the workmen on the roof, and Finn looked up quizzically.

'Solar panels,' I said. 'Carl says we're going to make enough power to feed some back into the grid.'

'Sweet,' said Finn, still standing there with his box full of birds and an *are you going to invite me in* look on his face.

'Oh, you can leave the box on the porch if you like. Come in, Finn. You can meet my mum.'

Finn turned out to be one of those friends who are especially good at making parents like them, which you have to admit is a pretty handy life skill. He even drank herbal tea, which really rocked Mum's world because she's so used to kids who argue all the time about who finished all the juice. To top it off, Finn asked Mum all about her work. I mean, what friend ever does *that*? Come to think of it, even *I* don't. It was as though Finn actually *liked* talking to my mum. Weird.

'Yikes!' I said, remembering Willow was still shut in the library. 'Come on, Finn, I'll show you around. You haven't even met Willow yet.'

Finn put his empty cup on the sink, which you could tell Mum also found dead impressive. 'Thanks for the tea, Mrs ... um ...'

'Aberdeen,' said Mum. 'Lovely to meet you, Finn. Call again, any time.'

After a quick tour of downstairs and a few Willow tricks we went up to the turret, which Finn liked best of all, mostly because of the telescope.

'Neat!' he said taking off the lens cap. 'When I finish school I'm going to study astrophysics.' He squinted

126

through the eyepiece. 'Wow, this is a *really* powerful telescope. I bet you can even see Pluto. Can you?'

I was a little embarrassed to say that so far all I'd used the telescope for was to spy through Settimio's windows or to check for vampire bats in the cypress trees. I hadn't really considered using it to look for *planets*.

'It's been so cloudy lately,' I said, neatening some books on my shelf. Do you like Harry Potter? I don't.'

'How could you *not* like Harry Potter, Sunny Hathaway?'

'I don't know, every time I read it, I fall asleep. I used to think maybe it was because of the spells. Please don't tell anyone, okay? Maybe I just need to start again from the beginning, or read it in the mornings.'

'You don't *have* to like it, Sunny.'

'Well, to me, it kind of feels like you do. *Everyone* does.'

Finn disconnected himself from the telescope and looked out the window to the river. 'Is that your boat?'

'Not mine personally; it came with the house. It's called *Queenie*.'

'Mad!' said Finn. 'Have you taken it down the river?'

'Not yet, we've pretty much just moved in. We can though – Mum said it's doesn't take that long to get into town. It's got a little motor, like a lawnmower.'

'Mad!' said Finn again.

'Not today though, 'cos we've got a business starting after lunch. Involving dogs.'

I was feeling a little pressured about maybe having totally run out of things to say. I mean, we'd done Pluto, Harry Potter and river boats. None of those topics exactly led to others. When I'm with Claud I never have to worry about thinking of stuff to say, on account of her being such a chatterbox. Then I remembered the whole purpose of Finn's visit.

'Hey, Finn, are we going to set those pigeons free?'

We set the crate on a patch of lawn near the rose garden at the front of the house. Willow was safely locked up in the library again and was peering through the window with her ears all pricked. I knelt down low so that I could see inside the cage. There were six pigeons in total. Two white, two greyish and two speckled reddish-brown ones.

'It's now or never,' said Finn undoing the latches on the wooden lid. Then he swept it open and we both stood back a little.

One of the white ones hopped up and perched on the side of the crate for a moment, while the others just looked about. Finn waved his hand gently around the cage and all of a sudden all six birds took off, making a whirring-whistling noise with the flapping of their wings. I looked so high above me that my neck hurt. Soon the whistling and whirring grew faint and their fluttering shapes became tiny specs against the clouds. Then they were gone.

Nowhere. Well, nowhere from my perspective, anyway.

But for them – they were busily flapping around *somewhere*. Somewhere up there they were finding their way home.

And that's the bit I couldn't understand about Granny Carmelene. Where actually was she for her, if she was nowhere for me? She had to be *somewhere* for her, didn't she?

Finn checked his watch. 'It's exactly ten-thirty,' he said, taking a notebook and pen out of his inside jacket pocket.

I kept looking up to the nowhere sky and out of the corner of my eye I saw a single pure-white feather spiralling and zigzagging towards me. I held out my hand and it landed gently on my palm, as if it was meant only for me.

'Do you believe in angels, Finn?' I asked, without even really meaning to.

''Course I do, Sunny Hathaway,' he said. 'What sort of guy do you take me for?'

'Have you ever actually seen one?'

''Course I have, Sunny Hathaway. I even met one on a bus one day. Crazy angel got herself all tangled up in my wool.'

17.

I forced myself to hold off from feeling too weird until after Finn had gone. I mean, I'd known *I* was suffering all the symptoms of an official pre-crush, but up until then I hadn't had any solid evidence that Finn might have a pre-crush too. But what he said about thinking I might be an angel *was* solid evidence, right? Even if it did make me blush, as well as remind me of how I'd nearly ruined his knitting.

I walked Finn down to the front gate and Willow trotted along after us, trying to grab a nibble of the white pigeon feather I was holding in my left hand. When we got to the gate, I leant down and held her by the collar, which was kind of handy because if Finn *did* happen to make another comment that made me blush I could easily hide my awkwardness by crouching down.

'So,' said Finn, holding up two twisted-together fingers. 'Here's hoping they all make it home.' He was safely on the other side of the gate with his empty pigeon crate.

'I'm sure they will, Finn,' I said, holding up the feather. 'But it's a pity you can't call me up and let me know, *or* SMS, *or* email.'

'Just you wait, Sunny Hathaway, once the pigeon post is up and running you'll—'

'Oh look,' I said, pointing over Finn's shoulder. 'You get to meet the precookeds.'

Lyall and Saskia were making their way up the hill, and it was perfectly obvious from Saskia's stompy walk and pokey-outy bottom lip that she and Lyall had been arguing. Again.

'Seriously, you guys!' I called out. 'You're like an old married couple!' I could tell Finn was trying not to laugh, which gave me the urge to try and say something even funnier at Lyall and Saskia's expense, but I managed to resist the temptation to avoid putting myself in the same smart-alec category as someone like Buster Conroy.

'Hey,' said Lyall, still puffing from the steepness of our hill. 'You must be Finn.'

I was hoping like crazy Lyall wasn't about to say something cringeable like *Sunny's told us ALL about you*, so I had to make absolutely sure he didn't get the chance.

'Lyall, Saskia, this is Finn. Finn, this is Lyall and Saskia. Finn's just heading off, aren't you, Finn? We just set his pigeons free, didn't we, Finn?' Finn looked a little overwhelmed. 'Come on Finn, I'll walk with you to the bus stop.'

'Hey, Sunny, don't be long,' said Lyall. 'We've got something to show you in the library.'

I knew *exactly* what he was talking about. The surveillance gear. And I'd been starting to think that maybe proof wouldn't be such a bad idea after all – if it made something become certain and all, like it had just become certain that Finn had a pre-crush too. It kind of makes you feel you can get on with stuff, and not just wonder about your wonderings all day.

Maybe if we did manage to catch an angel on Lyall's surveillance monitor it would somehow give me some relief from wondering so much about the whereabouts of Granny Carmelene? Don't ask me how. But you have to agree it was worth a try.

When I got back from the bus stop, Willow was waiting for me on the other side of the gate with a *You could have taken me with you* look on her face.

'I know, Willow, I'm sorry.' I said, squeezing my way back inside. It was weird. I had only just said goodbye to Finn, but I was already looking forward to seeing him again. And I didn't even know when that would be. Why hadn't I made a solid arrangement?

Suddenly I couldn't care less about the surveillance system, or Boredom Control either, for that matter. I just wanted to escape up to the turret, lie on my bed, close my eyes and have all the conversations I'd just had with Finn, all over again. Weird.

Willow started barking and made a couple of pounces towards me, crouching down on all fours and then darting away again.

'You're right, Willow!' I said. 'There's only one thing for it.' And I made a pouncing movement back at her, followed by one arms-outstretched twirl, throwing in a quick glance towards the library to make sure Lyall and Saskia couldn't see.

Willow did two spins and then barked to make sure I was planning on gearing up for more.

'Go girl!' I said, twirling about. She copied me exactly but in the opposite direction. 'We got to Washing Machine this crush business right out of me!'

'See how I've taped the wire around the doorframe?' said Lyall, pointing out his handiwork. 'It runs along the top of the skirting boards, around the corner and up the stairs.'

I went out to the entrance hall. 'Good job, Lyall,' I said. 'You can't see the wires at all.'

Lyall was obviously super-proud of himself and was talking at a million miles an hour. 'Then, at the top of the stairs, I've wired it under the hallway runner and into my room so we can keep check on the monitor, which, for now, is hidden under my bed.'

'Mad,' I said, checking my watch. 'Don't we have to go get the dogs soon?'

Lyall glanced over to his clock-radio.

'Crikey!' he said. 'We've got to go right now!'

Saskia was in the entrance hall with Willow, who had no idea that life as she knew it was about to be invaded by three strange dogs. What if they didn't get along?

'Did you see the *dogstacle* course we made, Sunny?' said Saskia. 'Don't you wish we'd thought of that name when we made the brochures?

'Ha! That's funny,' I laughed, feeling comforted by the idea that if Woolfie, Banjo, Sophia and Willow *didn't* get along, at least Willow would be able to outrun the others to safety. She was looking at me hopefully, as if it might be time for a walk.

'Sorry, Willow,' I said as we squeezed out the front gate and into the street. 'But we'll be back really soon with a *big* surprise.'

Kara Bleakly had given us a key, but I could see that she was home because her car was parked out front, so I buzzed on the intercom instead of letting myself in. Lyall and Saskia had gone off to get Woolfie and Banjo. Sophia's snout appeared instantly under the gate and she took three big snorts as I heard Kara's voice over the intercom.

'It's Sunny,' I said into the speaker. 'From Boredom Control.'

'Just push the gate, Sunny,' said Kara.

I tried to make my way up the front path but Sophia lunged at me, wagging her tail, her head and every other waggable part of her wide-load body.

'Down, Sophia,' I said, acting all stern as Kara appeared at the front door. I was actually worried Sophia might knock me over.

'She really needs to lose some weight,' laughed Kara. 'She's like a freight train.'

Someone once told me that dogs and their owners end up looking the same, or perhaps it's that owners choose the dog versions of themselves. But that sure wasn't the case with Kara Bleakly and Sophia. Apart from their black hair they were complete opposites. While Sophia was all happy, round and clumsy, Kara was pinched-in, wiry and without a hair out of place.

'Here's her leash, Sunny,' said Kara. 'Just leave her inside the gate when you get back. I'll put her dinner out because I'll be working late again tonight.' Kara bent down and gave Sophia a rub. 'You be a good girl now, won't you?' she said, and Sophia nodded her whole body in agreement.

When I got back to Windermere, Lyall and Saskia were already there with Banjo and Woolfie, and Willow was doing the Washing Machine interspersed with high-speed laps around the house. As I introduced Sophia, I caught a glimpse of Settimio peering out from his lounge-room window and disappearing again behind the curtain. I realised that the small amount of ground I'd made in getting him to like me had most likely been completely obliterated.

Once Willow had calmed down a little, we gathered all four dogs into a group at the front of the house and let them sniff each other to say hello. Luckily, there was tail wagging all round.

'Okay,' said Lyall, as if he was taking a PE class. 'First we're going to play Race Around the House, then we'll see how they go with the dogstacle course.'

'When can we start teaching them tricks?' asked Saskia, holding Willow's collar so that she didn't set the dogs off too soon.

'Later,' said Lyall, which if you ask me was sibling talk for *never*.

'I'll run ahead and get the race going,' I said. 'Just give me a few seconds head start before you let them off their leashes!'

Lyall and Saskia had all four dogs in sitting position: big tall Woolfie with his old-man scratchy grey hair; Banjo, all red and grey with his mischievous glinty eyes; Sophia, shiny smooth and black; and Willow, barely able to contain the excitement of having new friends.

I took off as fast as I could across the front garden.

'Ready…Setty…SPAGHETTI!' shouted Saskia behind me, and I presumed it was at the *spaghetti* part that she and Lyall let all four dogs run free. Within milliseconds Willow had outrun me, and Woolfie wasn't far behind. The two of them disappeared out of sight down the side of the house. That's when I glanced back and noticed Banjo, and how he wasn't at all interested in chasing Willow and Woolfie. Nor was he interested in Sophia, who had darted off in exactly the opposite direction. What Banjo was absolutely and undeniably interested in … was me!

He started barking and barking and darting to and fro in front of me, trying to cut me off. 'Shoo, Banjo!' I yelled. 'Go catch up with the others.'

He took one almighty lunge and nipped me square on my stripy-socked ankle. The pain, I tell you! *'Ouuuuuuuch!'*

Willow and Woolfie raced up behind me and ran past for another lap. Banjo didn't even notice them. He didn't take his eyes off me, but crouched low, ready to pounce again if I moved even a muscle.

'Lyaaaaaaaalll!' I hollered. 'Saaaaaaaaaskiaaaaa! Will somebody get this dog AWAY from me! Willow!'

But it was no use. Lyall and Saskia had taken off after

Sophia and were already down by the dogstacle course. I figured that if I stayed statue-still, Banjo might get bored and run off to the join others.

But no, it seemed Banjo was willing to keep guarding me endlessly. I made myself so still that I could have qualified as a museum exhibit. 'Shoo, Banjo!' I said, without even moving my lips.

Then I noticed Settimio hobbling through the orchard on his crutches, holding his plastered leg away from the wet grass. You could actually *see* the cogs of Banjo's mind ticking over, thinking he should round the both of us up into one cluster. He darted away from me over to Settimio and made a good solid lunge at Settimio's ankle.

For an old guy, Settimio sure had good reflexes. He managed to whack Banjo right across the nose with the end of one of his crutches, making Banjo run off yelping.

'*Cane stupido!*' Settimio called out after him.

And I said, 'Stupid dog!' Just in case Banjo couldn't understand Italian.

'Thanks, Settimio,' I said, bending down to inspect my ankle, which still hurt like anything and was even oozing blood.

'Come with me, Sunday. You need alcohol spirit for disinfecting. I fix for you.'

Settimio's cottage was toasty warm, and as he sat me down at the kitchen table I promised myself I wouldn't spy

138

on him any more through Granny Carmelene's telescope.

It seemed kind of strange: an old man on crutches with a bandaged nose patching up a kid with a hole in her ankle, and it occurred to me that I still didn't know how Settimio had hurt himself in the first place. He was filling a small bowl with water and soaking a wad of cotton wool when I asked him.

'I can't tell you, Sunny. You might laugh at me.'

'Really, Settimio, I wouldn't laugh. That'd be rude,' I said taking off my sock and rolling up my jeans a little. You could see one big Banjo tooth-hole with a bruise already forming around it.

'Maybe I tell you another time,' he said, dabbing the wound clean. 'I'm sure your grandmother laughs, too. God bless her soul.'

And I was tempted to ask Settimio exactly where he thought she was laughing, but I managed to restrain myself in case my question resulted in tears. I wasn't certain if those tears would be just mine either, nor whether Bruce and Terry could find me all the way out in Settimio's cottage.

To be successful in completely changing the topic, I focused my attention on the stone mantle above his kitchen fireplace. There were all sorts of little ornaments up there, as well as a candle burning, a small arrangement of roses from the garden and a photo of Granny Carmelene.

'Is how I honour her memory,' he said. Then he upturned

a brown glass bottle onto a fresh wad of cotton wool and positioned himself on the chair next to mine.

'This hurt a little bit maybe,' he said as he dabbed it on my sore ankle.

He was right; it hurt.

But luckily I was distracted by the sound of Saskia screaming hysterically from down by the river.

I jumped up and looked out the window. It was Sophia. She was right in the middle of the river all right, dog paddling around in circles. Lyall and Saskia were kneeling on the jetty trying to encourage her to swim back to shore. Before I could even think about getting my shoes back on I saw Woolfie and Banjo jump in after her. The only sensible dog was Willow, who (understanding that her skinny greyhound legs would be totally naff at dog paddle) had positioned herself safely on the jetty, where she could bark along with the others.

'Do something, Lyall!' I heard Saskia shouting. 'All our customers are going to drown!'

'I've got to go, Settimio,' I said. 'Thanks so much for the rescue mission.'

'Is okay, Sunny. But you should show your mother. You maybe need to visit doctor for injection.'

I smiled inwardly at the idea of actually volunteering information that might possibly lead to getting an injection. Was he for real?

'Good idea, Settimio,' I lied. 'I'll tell Mum as soon as she finishes work.'

By the time I got down to the river, Lyall and Saskia had all three dogs out of the water and back on their leashes.

'Gee, guys,' I said. 'Thanks for all your concern.' I showed them my ankle. 'Banjo's a delinquent; I vote he gets expelled from Boredom Control. And these are my favourite socks, too. Ruined!'

'Ow, Sunny,' said Saskia in empathy. 'I had no idea you got bitten.'

'Come on,' said Lyall. 'We've got to give him another chance. I'll handle him better next time, I promise.'

Carl seemed to be in a super-good mood at dinner that night. He didn't even notice that Saskia licked her knife with practically every mouthful, or that I fed most of my broccoli to Willow under the table.

'So, Lyall,' Mum said. 'What did the Archers' have to say about Banjo when you dropped him back. Did you happen to mention that he'd *bitten* Sunny?' (I'd had to tell Mum about the bite, but luckily she hadn't jumped on the injection idea.)

'Sort of,' said Lyall sheepishly.

Mum gave him an impatient glare. What exactly does *sort of* mean, Lyall? What did you *sort of* say?'

'Just that Banjo was very *spirited*,' Lyall said, making a focused effort to avoid eye contact with absolutely everyone.

'*Spirited*?' I shouted. 'He's *mental*, Lyall.'

'Aw, come on, Sunny, it was our first day. I didn't want to lose business. Banjo will settle down. We'll do some obedience training.'

'The whole thing was a disaster, Lyall. It's all right for you, you didn't get a hole in your ankle. Boredom *Control*? Give me a break; we had no control at all.'

'And we didn't even get to use the dogstacle course,' said Saskia.

'At least we got a new member for the environment group. When I dropped Woolfie back, Ritchie said he'd come for sure,' said Lyall, trying desperately to find a positive angle.'

Mum and Carl both looked delighted.

'Well done, Lyall,' Mum said. 'We really appreciate your help. Don't we, Carl?'

'I'm seriously thinking Boredom Control isn't the business for me,' I broke in. 'Entrepreneurs shouldn't have to deal with dog bites. That's what postmen are for.'

'Richard Branson's a billionaire entrepreneur,' said Saskia, enthusiastically. '*And* he's dyslexic.'

'Care factor zero, Saskia,' said Lyall. 'Unless someone comes up with a better idea, we're sticking with Boredom

Control. You can't bail before we've even properly started. Can she, Dad?' Lyall knew Carl would have to agree with him because he's always banging on about commitment and *seeing things through.*

'Lyall's right,' said Carl. 'At least see it through as a good holiday job.'

Later in the evening, when were supposed to be in bed, Saskia and I snuck into Lyall's room. He had the surveillance monitor set up on his desk and the screen was alight with a full view of the library. It was perfectly silent and black-and-white, like an old movie.

'We'll just sit and wait,' said Lyall. 'Like detectives.'

'Who's in charge of coffee and doughnuts?' I asked as I picked up a book (*Slam* by Nick Hornby) that was next to Lyall's bed. 'When did you get this?'

'Ritchie said I could borrow it,' said Lyall. 'He's such a cool guy. When I dropped Woolfie home he showed me inside. He's got a huge plasma and one of those fridges with an icemaker.'

'You just don't get it, do you, Lyall?' I said. 'The guy simply *can't* be cool if he wears Crocs. *Cool Crocs*. It's an oxymoron.'

'I agree,' said Saskia, sitting down beside me and leaning against Lyall's bed. 'What a moron!'

Lyall punched Saskia's arm. 'She said oxymoron, stupid.'

'Ow! I don't care what sort of moron he is.'

'Anyway,' said Lyall, 'When did Kara Bleakly become an authority on what's cool? So what if she doesn't like Crocs. She's just a hung-up kind of person.'

'She is not hung-up,' I said. 'I think she's just a little lonely.'

'Shh! said Saskia, still clutching her arm. 'Look!'

There was movement on the monitor as Mum and Carl came into the library. Willow followed close behind and immediately lay down in front of the fire. Mum had a folded newspaper under her arm and sat down on one of the reading chairs.

'Oh no,' I said. 'They're going to do the crossword. They'll be there for hours!'

'Boring!' said Lyall. 'Dad's even got his glasses on.'

'I'd seriously rather watch washing dry,' I said.

'Or grass grow,' piped in Saskia.

'Or do Theodore Costa's homework,' I said.

'Or go to confession,' said Saskia.

'As if an angel is going to appear in front of two middle-aged crossword junkies and a greyhound,' said Lyall.

Mum had opened the paper out onto a small side table next to one of the reading chairs. Carl warmed himself by the fire for a moment before suddenly taking off his glasses. He stood right in front of Mum's chair. She was madly scrawling a clue she'd obviously just cracked on

144

the crossword grid. It looked as though she hadn't even finished the word when Carl grabbed the pen out of her hand.

We couldn't hear what she said, but you could tell she was annoyed as. Carl held out his hand and took one of hers, pulling her up out of her chair. He led her over to the fireplace and nudged Willow out of the way with one foot. Then, still holding Mum's hand, he reached into his pocket, as if he were looking for some small change. Out came a small box.

'Get *out* of here!' said Lyall. 'Is Dad, like, *proposing?*'

If *we* were the ones who were being spied on right then, instead of Mum and Carl, you would have seen three kids all in a row, with their jaws dropped and their mouths wide open.

'Turn it off!' I said, but at the same time I really didn't want to, and it was too late because Carl was taking a ring out of the box and you could tell Mum said something like, *It's just beautiful.*

'Oh my god, he actually *is* proposing!' I said.

'Ewwww!' squealed Saskia. And then, 'Turn it off!' And then, 'Bags be flower girl!'

For a few moments I was frozen still. What were the odds of seeing that, right in the middle of trying to prove the existence of angels? Who would have thought? We just sat there staring, all three of us.

145

Until – you guessed it – Mum and Carl started kissing! Can you imagine? It was enough to have me on my feet in an instant pulling the plug to that surveillance monitor clean out of the wall.

18.

When I got back up to bed I found that my pillow had become a Willow. She was lying on it, fast asleep.

'Willow!' I said, clapping my hands. 'Off!'

She jumped down, looked at me guiltily for a moment and flopped onto the floor with a groan. She was asleep again in seconds.

I turned my pillow over to the other side and lay down. I was feeling a little strange, not that Mum marrying Carl would change anything much; we were already a blended family. There was just something about it being made *official*. Lyall and Saskia would by my *official* stepsiblings and Carl would be my *official* stepfather. You can't blame me for feeling a little uneasy. I mean, what if my stepfather turned bad? You read about it all the time in the paper.

And don't parents understand that kids might need things to be a little more gradual? Like how you grow out of your favourite jeans so slowly that you don't even notice. And what if Saskia *does* get to be the flower girl? This is *my* mother we're talking about, not hers.

I wasn't exactly jumping for joy, I can tell you, and really not looking forward to doing fake jumping for joy when Mum and Carl broke the news (probably at breakfast), and we had to pretend we had no idea. Or, worse still, if they acted all considerate and concerned and asked how we all *felt* about it, as if what we thought was actually going to change anything anyway.

By morning, Willow had snuck back up on the bed and was curled into a greyhound-ball at my feet. I had a panicky feeling that I was missing out on something. It was only when I caught a waft of cooking smells that I knew it was true. Pancakes!

'Come on, Willow,' I said, sweeping off the covers. 'Pancake frisbee, your favourite thing!'

The problem with Willow sneaking up to my room at night wasn't just that she got on the bed. It was also that she was still scared of going downstairs. I'd pulled my slippers on and thumped down to the landing before I noticed Willow hadn't followed me.

'Come on, girl!' I called, but she didn't appear. All I

heard was sulking from the top of the narrow stairs. I ran back up, taking the stairs two by two.

'Willow,' I said, standing at the bottom of the turret stairs. 'You've got down there heaps of times.' But she just made a whiny noise and barked at me.

'Willow, you have to *learn* how to get downstairs. What if there was a fire?' I said, climbing back up to the top. 'I'll do it just this one last time, but that's it. Promise?'

I promise, said Willow by the way she wagged her tail, along with her whole bendy body.

It wasn't so easy to carry a greyhound down two flights of stairs, I can tell you. Especially as I had to keep one arm on the hand-rail. I reached around under Willow's chest and she held her legs straight down, all stiff, like a wooden rocking horse. I had to put her down halfway and readjust my grip. 'I mean, seriously, Willow,' I said heaving her up again, 'this is just not dignified.'

But Willow didn't seem to mind at all. It was like when she was a puppy and I used to push her around in my old pram. She loved it, and didn't mind one iota if other dogs were watching.

'Seriously, Willow, imagine if any of your dog relatives could see you now.'

'Here she is,' said Mum, when I finally made it to the kitchen.

I suddenly remembered that she and Carl might be

going to make some type of cringeable announcement about *the engagement*. I managed to shoot a glance over Mum's left hand to see if there was a new piece of jewellery on her ring finger, but there wasn't.

Lyall and Saskia were sitting at the table eating pancakes, and they both gave me *the eyebrow* as if to let me know I wasn't the only one to think of doing a ring check.

'Morning, Sunny,' said Carl. He was looking at the answers to yesterday's cryptic. 'Well, whoever this DA person is, I just don't like him.'

He was talking about the initials that the crossword author signs under each grid. Mum and Carl were sadly so addicted to crosswords that they even had their favourite crossword authors, even though they knew nothing about them other than their initials.

'Really, *parmesan*, what's that got to do with *plateau*? Seriously, darl, if you and I actually met DA I can tell you right now, he's just not our sort of person. Oh, and for crying out loud, look at six across. *Dead Reckoning*, how is *anybody* meant to get that?'

'Morning, Carl,' I said, checking if there was enough pancake mixture left for me. 'Can I go next?' I cut a splodge of butter and watched it sizzle in the pan. I was planning on making a super-thin one for me and a good thick one for Willow. I was also planning on making sure there were no awkward silences, just in case Mum and

Carl tried to fill one with their *announcement*.

'Sunny, I thought we could sort through some of Granny Carmelene's things today. It would be nice to get that room set up for guests, and we can store anything you like up in the attic.' Mum helped me adjust the flame on the stove.

'What about you two?' said Carl to Lyall and Saskia. 'How about giving me a hand in the garden? We've got to get all those vegie beds mulched so they'll be ready for spring.'

'Um, I'm going to a friend's, Dad,' said Lyall.

'So am I, Dad, honest,' said Saskia. 'What did you two do last night?'

Both Lyall and I gave Saskia a look, while Mum and Carl smiled coyly at one another and looked all embarrassed. Then Mum started clearing the table without even telling me it was my job.

'Oh, we just relaxed in the library,' replied Carl. 'Didn't we, darl?'

Willow was under the table, resting her head on my leg as I finished my pancake (with butter, brown sugar, cinnamon and lemon), because she knew that hers would be coming next. I got up and sizzled some more butter in the pan.

Willow's pancake was thick and fat and I let some extra butter soak into it before making a dash for the back door with Willow right behind me nudging my bum. She ran down the back steps onto the grass.

'One, two, three!' I said, and flung the pancake frisbee as far as I could without making it break. Willow darted out and circled around and around, looking up in the air, until she heard it land in the middle of the frosty grass. I don't think Willow's eyesight is too good, even though she belongs to a class of dogs called sight hounds. She pounced on the pancake and it disappeared in two swift gulps. Then she ran straight back to me and sat up tall at my feet, hoping to have another turn.

'That's it, Willow. Sorry. Pancake frisbee is the world's shortest game.'

I'd successfully managed to avoid Granny Carmelene's bedroom since moving to Windermere. It was spooky as, and all still set up just as though nothing had ever happened. It made me feel as if she could walk back in at any moment, in one of her perfectly co-ordinated outfits.

I tell you, it was lucky I'd managed to summon Bruce and Terry up to the turret just beforehand, because if I hadn't just been heavily doused in grief repellent there was no way I could have been in that room at all.

Even so, when I looked at Granny Carmelene's big old bed all I could think about was her lying there all alone after writing me that letter, knowing she was about to die and not even being one bit scared about it.

Which got me thinking again about the topic of somewhere and nowhere and exactly *where, where, where* a person passes *to*, when they pass away. Away *where*?

'Come on, Sunny,' Mum said, sweeping open the curtains. 'Let's make a start.' She opened one of the windows to let in some fresh air.

'Do you believe in heaven, Mum?'

'Oh, Sunday, let's try and stay focused. I thought we could start with the dressing room.' She pulled back the sliding door. 'It's like a vintage clothing store in here.'

'Just asking,' I said, stepping inside.

Granny Carmelene's dressing room was long like a corridor, but a lot wider. On one side there were two levels of hanging racks, and the other side was floor-to-ceiling shelves, drawers, and pigeon holes for shoes and bags, which made me think of Finn and whether his pigeons made it home.

At the far end was a huge mirror all carved and decorated around the edges, which Mum told me was made of Venetian glass. To the right of the mirror was a door to Granny Carmelene's bathroom, which had a huge French porcelain bath that Carl said none of us were ever allowed to use, because of the water crisis.

I was flicking through a rack of summer dresses. 'Mum, I don't want to get rid of anything, 'cos when I'm older all this stuff might be in fashion again, and even if it isn't, I'm going to wear it anyway.'

'I agree,' said Mum. 'That's why we've got to store it all properly. I've got lots of boxes and tissue paper and some special silica packs to absorb any moisture. Oh, and some cedar and lavender balls to stave off the insects. That way you won't be getting around smelling all mothbally, like an op shop.'

'Ew, I hate that smell,' I said. 'Claud's grandma smells like that.'

Granny Carmelene had the bestest-ever shoe collection. Practically every single pair still had its own shoebox, and a handbag to match. I picked one up to check the size.

'Forty,' I said. 'So that's about a size nine, isn't it? What size are you, Mum?'

'I'm an eight. Don't worry, Sunny, you'll get no competition from me. They're all too big. Believe me, I've tried.'

That was a relief, I can tell you, because if there's one person you don't want to compete with in a clothing kind of way, it's your mum. My friend Ruby has that problem. Her mum's always buying the same clothes as her and dressing like a teenager. Ruby hates it. She just wishes her mum would wear Country Road.

I stood and stared at the rows and rows of Granny's shoes, all beautifully made to last for years. And I thought about Crocs, and how shocked and disappointed Granny's shoes designers would be if they knew that most of the world was wearing buckets on their feet nowadays.

'Can't we just leave it all stored in here?' I said. 'I mean, there's a perfect place for everything.'

'I know, love,' she said, taping up the bottom of a storage box. 'It seems perfect, but it's best for now to pack her things away. Besides, I'm sure Granny Carmelene would have wanted her things taken care of properly.'

As mum was speaking, I was looking in the mirror and imagining myself as an older, taller person (shoe size 40, of course), all dressed up in one of Granny Carmelene's outfits. I was at some sort of important occasion and Willow was with me on a leash that matched my bag. *Thank you, it belonged to my Grandmother*, I was saying to people who were giving me compliments on my super-stylish outfit. *Yes, it is lucky I turned out to be exactly the same size.*

It was precisely at that moment, when Mum had disappeared into the bathroom and I was floating off in my imagination somewhere between the present and the future, that I noticed a flickering up in one corner of Granny Carmelene's mirror. Just a flicker, and then it was gone, but a flicker clear enough for me to know what it was. The angel. Or should I say *my* angel, as it (she?) certainly only seemed to be interested in visiting me.

There was no point telling Mum, because I knew she wouldn't believe me. Or worse, she'd *pretend* to believe me because parents are meant to have faith in their own children, but she'd probably also be worried that I might be showing early signs of a mental illness.

'Sunny?' said Mum, tossing an empty box at my feet. 'We'd better get on with this, love.' She was stuffing one of Granny Carmelene's handbags with tissue paper to help it keep its shape.

'Mum, do you think angels are a way that dead people try to communicate with the people they've left behind?

'That sounds like the kind of question you'd be better off asking Auntie Guff.' She snapped the clasp on the bag closed and wrapped the whole thing up in soft fabric, before placing it carefully in a box.

Mum and I drifted into silence and packed and sorted all afternoon. We stacked the neatly sealed and labelled boxes on the landing for Carl to put up in the attic. We wiped all the shelves and put new liners in the drawers.

I had solid proof that Bruce and Terry's grief repellent only lasted about three hours, because the deep empty drawers of Granny Carmelene's dresser started reminding me of nothing other than a coffin. It was like a funeral all over again. I could tell Mum was sad too, but she didn't want to get bogged down it.

'There,' she said closing the window once more, as if a whole person's life could end up being explained by just one word.

There.

I flicked the light off in the dressing room and Mum and I both stood for a moment by the door, looking over the work we had done to try to make the room forget.

I thought about Granny Carmelene's things that I had up in bedside drawer – the locket, the photograph, the letter. And suddenly I wanted to get rid of them. I could throw the locket back into the garden and maybe even burn the photograph and the letter. People do that kind of thing all the time, you know.

But when I burst into my turret room, who should I find but Bruce and Terry standing by my open bedside drawer, where I also kept my letters from Finn!

'Don't worry,' said Bruce, 'we didn't read anything.' He handed me Granny Carmelene's things. 'You'd be making our lives a little easier if you dealt with these, Sunny.'

'No need to do anything drastic though,' Terry clarified. 'Maybe just shut 'em up in a box for a while, if you know what I mean.' He nodded towards the attic.

'Gotcha,' I said. 'Thanks, guys.'

But before I could thump downstairs to the attic-bound boxes marked *miscellaneous*, Terry grabbed me by the elbow and said, 'Wait. All this wondering and worrying you're doing about your grandmother – have you ever thought of just asking *her* where she is? I mean, you communicate with us, don't you?'

'Yes,' I said, feeling a little confused. 'But you're not dead. You're ... well you're ... you're Bruce and Terry.'

'That's right,' said Bruce. 'I'm Bruce and he's Terry.'

Terry rolled his eyes. 'Look, all I'm saying, Sunny Hathaway, is that there might be ways of communicating with them that's passed. Check with your googliser. It's as common as mud. Have a seance, Sunny, and put this whole mystery to rest.'

'Top idea, Terry,' said Bruce. 'A seance.'

'All in a day's work, my friend,' said Terry. All in a day's work.

'Ah ... Terry,' I said. 'Can you let go of my elbow now, please. I've got to go downstairs.'

Another letter from Finn was waiting for me on the kitchen table.

Dear Sunny Hathaway,

You'll be happy to know that all six pigeons arrived safely home. One of them was even back before I was! Have you tried seeing Pluto through your telescope yet? Maybe we could go to the Planetarium at Scienceworks and I can show you what to look out for. We could take the birds

there too, and they could have their first overseas trip.
Let me know what you think?
Your NFFFL
P.S. I really think you should try again with Harry Potter

But the fact was, it wasn't Pluto that really interested me. I mean, why can't there be a telescope powerful enough to see up to heaven? I'd be down at Scienceworks in a flash. At least then I could sort out whether or not heaven existed and if it did whether Granny Carmelene was up there. At least then I could cross *nowhere* off the list.

Maybe Terry was right. Maybe the one person I'd been forgetting to ask about her actual whereabouts was Granny Carmelene herself. It suddenly seemed so obvious.

I stayed up late that night researching on the internet, and I got to thinking about how Finn's letter had made me feel abnormal on two counts. One, for being the only person in the world who didn't like Harry Potter, and two, for being more interested in heaven than in Pluto. Still, I reckoned Finn could be persuaded to be interested in different planets, if you could call heaven a planet. I mean, what else could it be if it was floating up above?

And the way I saw it, Finn could also be convinced to maybe help me with some *other* things too, like seeing if you could communicate with the spirit world. If I pitched the idea well enough, spiritualism wasn't such a giant leap from astronomy. Was it? I mean, even President Lincoln used to get involved in seances, right there in the White House.

19.

It was Boredom Control time again and this time we thought we'd start with a treasure hunt. If the dogs were focusing on searching for treats, Sophia might not think about jumping in the river, and Banjo might have something better to do than try to round me up like a wayward cow, and Woolfie wouldn't dig up Settimio's roses.

Lyall had bought a pack of doggie tidbits from the pet shop and was portioning them out to Saskia and I like mixed lollies. Saskia made a trail around the house like in *Hansel and Gretel*.

'Won't this just make Sophia even fatter?' I said.

'Nah,' replied Lyall. 'Afterwards we'll work them out on the dogstacle course.'

While Lyall and Saskia were hiding the rest of the treats, I set off to Kara Bleakly's to pick up Sophia. Kara was just leaving the house when I arrived.

'Perfect timing, Sunny,' she said. 'Now I can leave without any dog-guilt.'

I stood in the gateway while Kara clip-clopped out into the street in her high heels. Kara sure did seem to work a lot. Surely it's not good for a person to live alone and not have enough time to make a new friend or even to walk their dog?

When I got back to Windermere, Lyall, Saskia, Woolfie and Banjo were already there.

'Where's Willow,' I said, handing Sophia's leash over to Saskia. Woolfie gave Sophia a big lick on the face and Sophia's tail wagged hard.

'We forgot to let her out of the house,' said Saskia.

Lyall was practising getting Banjo to sit on command, which seemed to be working, but I was still a little nervous for my ankles. Just to be safe, I was wearing my gumboots with Explorer socks.

Finally we were ready to let the dogs go. Sophia immediately found the trail and started systematically gobbling up each treat, but the other dogs couldn't have cared less. They were too busy chasing each other around the garden and doing giant laps around the house with

Willow striding at least ten dog-lengths ahead at all times, smiling from ear to ear.

'This is all wrong!' I said as Sophia followed her nose around the entire circuit, hoovering up all the treats as she went. She even knocked over the logs and found the treats I'd stashed underneath. 'Sophia needs to be running, not eating.'

'I'll see if she'll run with me,' said Saskia. Come on Sophia! *So-phi-a!*' Saskia took off towards the front of the house, but Sophia ignored her and kept sniffing about to see if there was anything else to eat.

Willow must have finally had enough of being chased because she sought me out and hid her head between my knees, puffing like anything. Banjo threw himself onto the grass to cool down, and Woolfie ran over to Sophia as if he'd suddenly realised there had been a treasure hunt and he'd missed out. Once Willow was satisfied there would be no more chasing, she too flopped down on the grass.

'It's no use,' said Saskia, making her way back. 'Sophia's just not the running around type.'

'Why don't we do a few laps of the house with Sophia on her leash?' I attached Sophia's leash and started jogging. 'Make sure you don't let Banjo follow!' I yelled over my shoulder.

Sophia trotted obediently beside me, and Woolfie did too, nibbling at Sophia's collar the whole way around. By the time we'd all had a turn Sophia was puffing and panting and I felt satisfied that she'd had some exercise, even if it was just to make up for the treasure hunt. At least we were back to square one.

Next we threw the ball for the other dogs. We were watching Woolfie, Willow and Banjo, so nobody noticed that Sophia had slunk away until we heard a loud splash from the river. This time, though, Saskia knew it wasn't a matter of life and death. And when we arrived on the scene, Sophia was happily swimming in circles.

'Maybe Sophia will swim after a stick,' said Saskia. 'Then it would be like she was swimming laps.' She found a straight arm-length stick near the water's edge and threw it as far as she could out into the river in front of Sophia.

Sophia *did* actually bring it back. Every time! which was a huge relief because if Sophia didn't start to slim down, Kara Bleakly would have no hesitation in giving us the sack.

For some reason neither Woolfie, Banjo nor Willow wanted to join Sophia in the water, but you could tell they were awfully impressed with the way she swam back with the stick, heaved herself out of the river, shook herself off (still with stick in mouth) and dropped the stick once more at Saskia's feet.

'You see that, guys?' Lyall said to Banjo, Woolfie and Willow. 'Now that's what you call *cooperation*.'

Woolfie's ears pricked up momentarily as if to say, *I'll show you cooperation*, and the very next time Sophia swam the stick back to the river bank, Woolfie leant over and gently took it from her, just like in a baton relay. Sophia turned and swam back out to the middle while Woolfie carried the stick over to Saskia and dropped it at her feet. We all cheered as if it was a trick Woolfie and Sophia had been working on for months.

'Way to go!' I yelled, still clapping as Saskia threw the stick out into the river again.

'Sophia and Woolfie really like each other,' said Saskia. 'It's a shame they can't hang out at each other's places when they're not at Boredom Control.'

'They could, I guess,' I said. 'If Ritchie and Kara knew each other existed.'

We went silent for a moment, possibly because we had all thought of the same incredibly good idea. If we were cartoon characters we would all have had light globes go on above our heads.

'Brilliant!' said Lyall. 'Boredom Control could add a whole new arm to the business: matchmaking. Do we charge extra for that?'

'Yay!' squealed Saskia. 'If Kara and Ritchie were friends, Woolfie and Sophia could be friends too!'

'And Kara and Ritchie might fall in love!' I said, not quite believing the pukie words that were coming out of my own mouth. I was already formulating the perfect plan – a way of Kara and Ritchie meeting where they wouldn't know they'd been set up. It was a slightly mischievous idea because it involved a little (just a little) meddling into other people's lives, but surely it was okay if it meant *helping* other people. Let's face it, Kara just wasn't going to find anyone on her own...

When it was time to drop the dogs home I put my idea into action. We gathered their leashes together, and right before Lyall clipped them on I took Sophia's and Woolfie's collars off and swapped them around.

'Brilliant!' said Saskia. 'Ritchie and Kara will have to talk to one another to get the right collars back, and their phone numbers are right there on the tags.'

'Nice work, Sunny!' said Lyall.

'Yes! I love it!' said Saskia, jumping up and down on the spot.

'But Woolfie's hair is so long,' added Lyall. Ritchie might not even notice he's got the wrong collar.'

'Kara will, believe me,' I said as we made our way towards the front gate.

'There is *one* problem though, Sunny,' said Saskia, as we were walking down our street. 'A bright green problem in fact.'

'*CROCS!*' we all said at once.

'Those tragic green crocs of Ritchie's could stand in the way of a life of a potential perfect match,' I said. 'They could possibly ruin the whole plan!'

'Don't worry, Sunny,' said Lyall, with a particularly devilish look on his face. 'You can leave that part up to me ...'

20.

On my way over to Dad and Steph's I posted a letter to Finn because I wanted him to come over again in three days time and you have to really plan ahead with snail mail. At least the pigeon post would be a little more efficient.

Dear Finn,

I'm glad the pigeons made it home and their electromagnetic homing devices didn't get interfered with by mobile phone towers, like you thought they might.

About Scienceworks — didn't you get to go with school? I've got a better idea. How about you help me try and communicate with the spirit of my recently deceased

Grandmother? You know, like have a seance. Then she could tell us where nowhere was, for her. Maybe you have an encyclopaedia or something you could look it up in, under 'S' for seance or it might also be under Spiritualism.

The thing is, I know my grandmother has to be somewhere because I'm fairly convinced she's been sending angel messengers. So anyway, Finn, I'm thinking we could have a seance. You, me, Saskia and Lyall, the sceptic. I haven't told them about it yet but by the time you get this letter I probably will have.

So, come over on Sunday at ten in the morning because I'm going to my Dad's for a little while now. Things are a bit grim over there but I'm determined to at least cheer Flora up a little.

Sunny Hathaway

P.S. I will start again with Harry because not being into it sure makes me feel like a grinch.

P.P.S If I don't hear from you I'll presume you think I'm a freak for suggesting a seance, so, sorry.

Finally, I was Flora-bound. She was all I could think about on the bus.

I kind of think I might know how it feels to be a mother because even though Flora is only my half-sister, it feels as if some sort of magnet is pulling me to be with her all the time. Being away from her just feels wrong and that's the only way I can explain it.

Living in two houses makes it worse. I mean, Flora's my half-sister *plus* I only get to see her *half* the time. Even I know that only adds up to a quarter, and Maths is my worst subject. I'm planning all the ways I'm going to make it up to her when she gets a little older. I'm definitely going to take her to the Melbourne Show and let her go on all the rides, instead of just looking at the animals like Mum did with me. And I'm definitely going to tell her about the existence of morning television and not keep it a secret like Mum did. Can you believe I only found out there were kids' shows on the tellie in the mornings when I started school? I should have definitely called the Kids Help Line about that one!

Auntie Guff's car was in the driveway when I got to Dad and Steph's. Dad's car was there too, which was weird because it was only four in the afternoon. I slipped my key into the lock and opened the door as quietly as I could, in case Flora was sleeping. Guff was in exactly the same position as she had been last time – cooking meals for the freezer.

'Sunny!' she said, washing her hands.

'Hey, Guff,' I whispered. 'What's cooking this time?'

'Well, it's one of those daggy old seventies favourites from the *Women's Weekly Cookbook* – apricot chicken.'

'Yum,' I said pulling open the pantry doors. 'I love a fork dish. Where is everyone? How come Dad's home already?'

'They had an appointment with the doctor. He's just outside, darl, hanging a load of washing out. And Steph's having a bit of a lie-down with the baby.'

As usual, I thought to myself, when it suddenly occurred to me that maybe it was only when *I* was around that Steph hid in the bedroom. Maybe she just didn't want to talk to *me*?

Dad came though the back door with the empty laundry basket. He looked kind of spooked and hollow, as if he might have even forgotten I was coming. I went over and gave him a hug.

'Hi, Dad. What's up?'

'Make us a pot of tea, would you, Sunny? We need to have a bit of a talk.'

Dad sat down at the kitchen bench while I got three cups from the cupboard and put the kettle on. Guff gave Dad *the eyebrow*, as if to say, *Do you want some help with*

171

this, because we all know having talks is really not your strong point?

I was starting to think I'd done something wrong, but I honestly couldn't think of anything. Well, apart from the telescope-stalking of Settimio and switching the dog collars, but as if Dad would know anything about that. In his eyes, I was a model citizen. Still, the very feeling of a big serious talk made me want to take a trip on *ThinAir*, but ever since the upgrade, even that didn't seem like an attractive option.

Dad poured three cups of tea and then cleared his throat.

'I took Steph to the doctor again today. You know how she's been having a difficult time of it? Well, I'll get straight to the point, she's been diagnosed with postnatal depression.'

'I don't get it,' I said, putting some honey in my tea.

'Hopefully it's a temporary thing,' added Guff, trying to sound positive.

'But I don't understand why Steph is even depressed in the first place. She was so excited about having Flora. Shouldn't it be a happy time, now that she's actually here?'

'It doesn't always work that way, I'm afraid,' said Dad. 'Steph just feels wretched, and guilty for feeling wretched and for not being able to enjoy Flora like she thought she would.' He was getting all teary-looking, which must have been contagious because pretty soon I was getting throat ache real bad.

'But what about Flora? Babies pick up on vibes, if you don't know, Dad.' I could imagine how bad it might feel to be a tiny baby and for your only mother in your only life to be all bent out of shape because you'd been born. I mean, Willow knows when I'm not happy with her and she's a dog.

Then I remembered how in Year Three we had to carry an egg around with us for a whole week so that we could get an idea of how demanding it was to be a parent. Maybe if Steph had done an experiment like that she might have discovered that she just wasn't cut out for motherhood. Maybe Steph's egg would have broken like Ruby Cantwell's, or maybe she might have lost it like Claud almost did. In any case, I was kind of cross with Steph, even though I was meant to be having *compassion*.

'So that's why Steph's been such a grump?'

'Sunday!' said Dad angrily, and Guff quickly stopped nodding.

'Sorry,' I said, wiping away a tear.

I buzzed for the hostess and she came in hardly any time at all because up in first class you have a hostess pretty much all to yourself.

'Yes, Sunday, would you like something to eat?'

'I think I'll go for the signature steak sandwich please. And can I have the relish on the side? I sometimes don't like chilli.'

'Coming right up Ms Hathaway, it won't be long at all.'

'Thanks so much, and after that I think I'll try the raspberry friand, the Gypsy cream biscuits and the chocolate-coated vanilla ice-cream. Oh, and just out of interest, whose signature do you get with the steak sandwich?'

I was brought back from the clouds by some baby squeaks coming from the bedroom, and Steph opened the door with Flora in her arms.

'I've just been having a talk with Sunny,' said Dad.

'Hi, Sunny,' said Steph, giving Flora to Dad. 'Sorry it's not exactly *uplifting* over here at the moment.' Steph flopped onto the couch.

'If you'd prefer I didn't come over for a while, I under—'

'No! Please,' said Steph, 'that would make me feel like a *total* failure.'

Flora's squeaks were becoming more and more unsettled.

'How about Sunny and I take her for a walk?' said Guff. 'Dinner's cooked. We just need to steam some rice.'

'You're a doll,' said Steph. 'She's just had a feed and

she's got a clean nappy, so with any luck, she just might drift off to sleep.'

Guff and I pushed Flora in the pram to Murray Park. I could remember Guff taking me there when I was small and how once I'd cried because my undies had got caught on the slide as I was going down and I got a front-wedgie.

Flora stayed awake, looking up at the sky, sometimes crinkling her forehead. It reminded me of when she was first born and I'd noticed she had little frown lines. Maybe she'd known her mum was about to catch depression. Why else would a baby look so worried?

Guff must have read my mind. 'Steph will be fine, Sunny. It will all be okay.'

'Well, I'm eleven and I feel unwelcome with Dad and Steph, so can you imagine how Flora must feel?'

'No one actually asks to get depressed; give Steph a break. And you're hardly unwelcome, Sunny. Besides, you and I have to be strong and stick together. Steph will pull through, don't you worry.'

I was getting a little tired of adults saying *don't you worry*. I mean, there was *plenty* to worry about. Why couldn't they see that?

Guff's apricot chicken was super-delicious, even if the rest of dinner was full of uncomfortable silences. I could tell that Steph was making an effort, even though she obviously didn't feel like talking. She must have really been scratching about for something to say because she finally resorted to asking the *How's school?* question, which is about as interesting as brussels sprouts?

'Um, it's school holidays,' I said, hoping not to make Steph feel bad for being out of touch with reality.

'Oh, it is too,' she said. 'I've lost all track of time.'

When Dad came to tuck me in later that night he hit me with *another* clanger. He had to go away for work for a while. To China.

'Under the circumstances, with Guff going away too, it's probably best that Steph and Flora go back to Perth where Steph's family can support her.'

'Perth! That's practically ten hours away. I'd *never* get to see Flora! No, Dad! You can't take Flora away! Especially with Steph not even really liking her.'

'Please don't say that Steph doesn't *like* Flora, Sunny. She loves her. It's just that she's under a dark cloud. Steph's needs have to come first here. Her sister is in Perth, and her parents. She needs family support. It's really important that you understand, Sunny, and try not to be judgemental

'I'll try,' I said reluctantly. It felt easier to be annoyed with Steph than to *understand* her. 'How long does postnatal depression last? Is there a cure?'

'I'm not sure,' said Dad. 'Each person is different. I guess it's like getting over a bad case of the flu. There's the part where you feel you're coming down with something; the part where it really hits you; the part where you just have to lie down, rest and sweat it out; and then the part where you slowly get stronger.'

It did help to imagine Steph having come down with something a little like a bad flu, but it didn't stop me worrying about Flora. She didn't have *any* way of trying to understand. Maybe I could invent a cure? Something to speed up Steph's recovery a little. I mean, look how well grief repellent had been working for me.

Dad pulled the covers up around my shoulders.

'I really wish you didn't have to go away, Dad,' I said as he gave me a goodnight kiss.

'Believe me, Sunny,' he said. 'So do I. Couldn't be worse timing.'

As I drifted off to sleep I had a crazy idea. Instead of Steph and Flora going to Perth, they could come and stay with us at Windermere while Dad was away. We could make Granny Carmelene's old room into a type of hospital where Steph could take all the time she needed to recover, and I could make sure Flora was all right because I'd be with her everyday. I wish.

21.

Maybe it was because she's got keen intuition, or maybe it was because I was quieter than usual, but the moment I got home to Windermere, Mum asked me if everything was okay over at Dad and Steph's.

'Postnatal depression?' she said, after I told her. 'Your father hasn't said a word to me about it.'

'It's an official diagnosis,' I said. 'From the doctor.'

Mum and I were in the kitchen preparing dinner. I was scrubbing potatoes at the sink and could see Carl out in the vegetable garden with a basket full of silverbeet and apples, munching on one he'd picked from Granny Carmelene's tree. Willow was sniffing along beside him, but she barged ahead when he opened the back door, and suddenly appeared in the kitchen wagging her tail.

'Have a look at these apples,' said Carl, putting the basket down on the bench near the sink. 'Completely chemical free; you just can't get better than that.'

Mum handed me a peeler. 'Could you do a few apples too, Sunny, after you've peeled the potatoes? We'll make a crumble for dessert.'

'Where are Lyall and Saskia?' I asked, hoping I wouldn't be the only one around to lend a hand.

'They should be here soon,' said Carl, checking his watch.

'Sunny was just telling me a little bad news, darling,' Mum said. 'Apparently Steph's got PND.'

'And,' I continued, 'the worst part is that Dad's going to China for at least a month, so Steph and Flora might have to go to Perth, and I wouldn't get to see Flora *at all*. It's not *fair*. Why did Dad and Steph spend months getting me all excited about having a baby sister if they were just going to take her away from me?'

'Sunny,' said Mum in her stern voice. 'Try not to see it as all being about you, darling. Steph is in crisis. No one *chooses* to have postnatal depression.'

'If you ask me,' said Carl, 'it's a direct symptom of the breakdown of the extended family network.'

'I agree,' said Mum. 'It's just not natural to be living in separate little houses with fences all around us. New mothers these days have got it tough. Home all day alone with a baby, completely cut off.'

'Which is why they say *it takes a whole village to raise a child,*' said Carl.

'Isn't Auntie Guff helping out?' said Mum, chopping the potatoes into wedges.

'Yes, she's made loads of frozen casseroles, but she's got a film shoot starting next week in South Africa.'

'I might go call your dad and Steph now,' said Mum, wiping her hands, 'and see if there's anything I can do to help. Where have you kids left the phone? Last time I found it in Lyall's bed.'

'Want to know what I think?' said Carl.

'What?' I said, thinking he was going to launch into a new idea to make silverbeet edible.

'I think your dad and Steph, and Flora of course, should all move in here.'

I froze mid apple-peel and Mum stopped dead in her tracks.

'It's not as silly as it sounds,' Carl continued. 'We've got plenty of room.'

'Yes!' I squealed in a very Saskia way. I dropped the peeler and without even thinking I found myself running over to Carl and giving him a hug. I almost blurted out something along the lines of, *You're going to be the best official stepfather ever, Carl!* Luckily I caught myself just in time. That really would have been a complete Saskia thing to do.

Mum looked a little flummoxed. 'I don't know,' she said. 'It's a nice idea, Carl, and it's fine by me, it really is, but moving in with your husband's ex-wife and her new family is not exactly everyone's cup of tea. Steph might *want* to be around her own family.'

'Can you at least just offer, Mum? Pleeeeeeeeeease?'

'Can't hurt to ask?' said Carl, handing Mum the phone, which he'd just found underneath a pile of newspapers.

By the time Lyall and Saskia got home it was official. Dad, Steph and Flora were coming to stay at Windermere. And when Dad went away, we'd look after Steph and Flora.

'Steph loved the idea,' said Mum over dinner. 'Amazing.'

'I *knew* she didn't really want to go to Perth,' I said. 'She told me once that the whole reason she moved to Melbourne in the first place was to get away from her family.'

'Cool! I love babies,' said Lyall.

'So do I,' added Saskia. 'Yum, these roast potatoes are the best, Alex.'

'Thank you, Saskia,'

'I peeled them,' I said.

Carl suddenly stood up and went to the pantry. He came back with five champagne glasses and put them carefully down on the table. Then he took a bottle from the fridge, tore off the wire and foil, and popped the cork. Mum looked all girlie and embarrassed and pretended she had to get something off the bench so that she could turn her back and no one would notice that she'd gone red.

'Well,' said Carl, filling up the glasses (us kids only got a thimbleful). 'I think we've got a couple of things to celebrate here.' He held up a glass of champagne for Mum.

'Come over here, love,' he said. 'Stand by me.'

Mum stood sheepishly next to Carl at the head of the table, staring at the bubbles in her champagne.

'Not only is it wonderful that we can offer our support to Steph and Flora, but we've also been waiting for the right moment to make a very important announcement,' said Carl. 'And we really do hope you're going to be as happy about it as we are.'

'You're engaged!' said Saskia, and Lyall punched her hard on the arm.

'Saskia, shhh,' Lyall said.

'Ow!' she cried. 'It was your idea, Lyall.'

'Lyall's idea to do what, exactly?' asked Carl.

Lyall gave Saskia an evil look. 'If you say what I think you're going to say, Saskia, you'll seriously regret it,' he said in a muffled voice.

'Will somebody tell us what's going on, please?' Mum stared directly at me. 'Sunny?'

'Don't look at me, Mum. It's your announcement.'

'Congratulations!' cried Saskia, raising her glass. 'Can I be flower girl?'

'Congratulations,' said Lyall, swigging his champagne before anyone else had even clinked glasses.

'For goodness sake, Lyall,' scolded Carl. 'I'm trying to make a toast here. You don't gulp it down!'

'Sorry, Dad. But, like, I *am* Australian. Can I have a bit more?'

'Certainly not! You can have water instead.' Carl filled Lyall's champagne glass with water, and Mum looked seriously confused.

'Talk about a non-announcement,' laughed Carl.

'Sunny?' Mum asked, trying to gauge my reaction, like how I do when I'm trying to read Willow's mind.

I went over and gave her a hug. 'I think it's great news, Mum.' I gave Carla quick hug too – the second one of the day. 'Congratulations, Carl.'

Then we all chinked our glasses together, and Carl said, 'To us,' and we all said, 'To us.'

Except for Lyall, who said, 'It's not fair that I have to make a toast with water.'

22.

I woke up feeling happy and excited but it wasn't about Mum and Carl getting married. It was more about how there was only one more sleep until Dad, Steph and Flora moved in, which meant I'd be living in just one house for the first time I could remember. Mum wouldn't get cross with me for leaving my basketball uniform at Dad's, and Dad wouldn't get cross with me for leaving my bathers at Mum's. And I wouldn't have to clog up my memory with thoughts about what belonged where. Can you imagine what I could do with all that new brain space?

It was perfect that Steph would be sleeping in Granny Carmelene's old room. Not only had Mum and I done a great job in making it into a guest room, but it's not everyday she got to stay somewhere with a built-in angel.

I could hear the clunking of the water pipes in the kitchen, and the deep tone of Carl's voice (most likely talking about crossword clues). I jumped out of bed and flew down the stairs.

Lyall and Saskia were both munching cereal, probably so as not to have to answer questions about how we knew about Mum and Carl's announcement before it was announced.

'Here she is,' said Mum.

'Morning, Sunny,' said Carl, looking up from the paper.

'Hey, Sunny,' said Lyall and Saskia. Lyall had a guilty look on his face and it wasn't long before I worked out why.

Carl stood up to make a coffee, and that's when I noticed the situation he had going with his feet. He was wearing a pair of puffy Explorer socks *and* a bright green pair of Crocs!

Carl must have noticed me giving them *the eyebrow*.

'Do *you* know where these came from, Sunny? No one else does. I found them stuffed in the bottom of the laundry basket.'

'I didn't put them there, if that's what you mean.' I threw a glance at Lyall.

He wouldn't catch my eye, because he knew I'd have given him *the eyebrow*, too.

'Well, it sure is a mystery,' said Carl. 'Maybe they're an engagement present from that angel of yours, Sunny?

'The thing I can't get over, apart from their mysterious appearance and the fact that they are so comfortable, is that they're *exactly* my size.'

'Maybe they're Settimio's?' said Mum. 'Maybe Willow brought them in from the garden?'

'Nope, I checked with Settimio. It's just one of those things – meant to be.'

'You're not going to wear them in public are you, Dad?' asked Lyall.

'Why the heck not?' said Carl. 'Everyone else does, and at this rate I don't think I'm likely to ever want to take them off. I just had no idea Crocs were this comfortable. No wonder they're a world-wide phenomenon.'

'So were Pokemon, Dad,' said Lyall. 'But we knew to resist them.'

'Yeah, and so is dyslexia,' said Saskia, 'but I'm not allowed to have *that*.'

'Don't be ridiculous, Saskia,' said Carl.

'Well it's all right for you, Dad! Your words don't swirl!'

'That reminds me,' said Mum. 'Ritchie called last night, and apart from asking me to let you know there had been some sort of mix-up with his dog's collar, he confirmed he'll be attending our next action-group meeting tomorrow night. Isn't that great? Thanks for spreading the word.

'That's *great*,' said Saskia and I together.

'Yep,' said Lyall, '*great*.'

'Good one, Lyall,' I said as soon as Mum and Carl had left the kitchen for Willow's morning walk. 'Pure genius.'

'Yeah, brilliant idea, Lyall,' mocked Saskia. 'The laundry basket. Nobody *ever* looks there. It's the *perfect* place to stash a pair of shoes that you've *stolen* from one of your own customers.'

'Don't start, Saskia,' said Lyall. I could tell he was holding back from punching her.

'Couldn't you have just hidden them in Ritchie's garden or under his verandah?' I said. 'That's what I thought you had in mind. When you said you'd take care of things.'

'I'll fix it,' said Lyall. 'I'll think of something.'

'That's what worries me. Meanwhile, my *only* mother is stuck with a guy who wears Crocs – *with* socks, Lyall, *socks*!'

23.

Later that afternoon, Mum and I picked a huge bunch of roses and put them in a vase in Granny Carmelene's old room. The room was all aired and vacuumed, with fresh new sheets and brand new soap, just like in a hotel.

'There,' said Mum fluffing up the pillows. 'We're all ready. It'll be lovely having a baby in the house again.'

'Mum? You can't let Carl get about in those Crocs. Can't you do something?'

'I stopped worrying what other people think years ago, Sunny. But having said that, I'm doing my best to get him out of them, believe me.'

'You should especially tell him not to wear them *tonight*, to the action group. I mean, who's going to take seriously someone who wears bright green Crocs?'

After dinner (Mum snuck disgusting capers into the tuna pasta – *again!*), Lyall and Saskia and I had to help set up for the action group. Carl was racing about stapling sheets of paper together and setting the whiteboard up in the library, and, yes, he was wearing Ritchie's Crocs. As soon as Ritchie walked in the door he would surely notice them. After we'd finished helping we had to find somewhere to spy. We had to *hear* what was being said, so Lyall's surveillance gear just wasn't going to cut it. Unfortunately, there was only one valid spot: the drawing room.

'No way!' said Saskia. 'I've been pretending that room doesn't exist.'

'It's either that or freeze to death on the verandah,' said Lyall. 'Just get over it. As if the paintings actually talk.'

'Lyall's right. Quick, before Mum and Carl see us.'

We herded Saskia into the drawing room and she ran over to sit in one of the green chairs. 'I'm going to be flower girl at the wedding,' she announced, as proud as a queen on a throne.

'You can't just *announce* that, Saskia. It's *my* mum.'

'Well it's *my* dad, Sunny, and he said I could be flower girl.'

Luckily, Saskia and I were distracted by the doorbell because otherwise we might have had our first fight.

'Shh!' Lyall said. 'It could be Ritchie.'

We peeked around the doorway into the entrance hall. Sure enough it was Ritchie, right on time. Mum and Carl were introducing themselves.

'Come in, Ritchie,' Mum said, ushering Ritchie towards the library. 'We're holding the meeting in here.'

'Thanks,' said Ritchie, following Mum and Carl into the library. 'Hey, nice shoes, Carl. You wouldn't believe it; I've got a pair *exactly* the same. Or I *had* a pair. Can't find them anywhere. They've just *disappeared*.'

Mum and Carl exchanged dubious frowns.

'No kidding?' said Carl suspiciously as the doorbell rang again. 'How strange.'

Don't ask me how he knew we were in the drawing room, but Carl darted in on the way to answering the door again.

'I need to have a *word* with you, please, Lyall,' Carl said in his authority voice.

Saskia and I both stared at the ceiling.

'Dad, the *door*,' said Lyall, trying to distract him.

'I'll give *you* the door. You've really done it this time and you'd better come up with a decent explanation. Do you have *any* idea how I feel wearing these shoes now? Did you honestly think no one would put two and two together?'

Carl closed the drawing room door firmly behind him, and Lyall slumped deep in his chair. He gave Saskia and I his best greasy look.

'Don't look at us!' I said. 'We had absolutely nothing to do with it.'

'*What*ever,' said Lyall.

It wasn't just the Crocs we got busted for. After Mum and Carl had seen the last person out they rounded us all up in Lyall's bedroom.

'Would someone please explain this?' Mum was holding Lyall's surveillance camera.

'Um, it's mine. I bought it with my Christmas money,' said Lyall. 'We were just, like, using it to conduct an experiment. Like in science.'

'*Science?*' repeated Mum.

'We were trying to see if angels exist,' Saskia said. 'Cos Sunny keeps seeing them.'

'So this is what you're doing when you're meant to be in bed asleep?'

'Only a couple of times,' I said. 'It's no big deal, Mum. Holidays and all.'

'Stealing people's shoes is though, isn't it, Lyall?' said Carl. 'Why on *earth* would you do that? You're going to buy Ritchie a new pair with your own money!'

'Daaaad! I'll put them back. I promise. Please don't make me tell Ritchie. It was just a stupid mistake.'

'What have you got to say for yourself, Sunny?' Mum was pacing up and down like some type of prison guard.

'It was kind of part of a bigger plan,' I said, hoping we could show her that we were actually trying to offer Ritchie and Kara a *community service*.

'You had a plan that involved stealing Ritchie's Crocs? Give me a break, Sunny!'

'Our plan needed Ritchie *not* to have any Crocs, if you know what I mean.'

'No, I *don't* know what you mean, Sunny,' said Mum. 'But I *am* waiting.'

Saskia filled Mum and Carl in about our matchmaking scheme and how it was never going to work if Kara found out Ritchie was a Croc-wearer.

'For goodness sake!' snapped Carl. 'If someone is going to be so shallow as to judge a person by their shoes, what hope have we got as a society?'

'I can kind of see their point though, darl,' said Mum. 'You've got to admit, Crocs on adults are hardly very – ah, how would you put it – hardly very *suave*.'

Carl look downright hurt.

'Now, Lyall, I'd like you to put Ritchie's shoes back ASAP. I'll run the darn things through the wash and you can do it tomorrow.'

'And the surveillance gear?' said Mum. 'You were spying on us the other night weren't you? That's why our big news came as no surprise. That's just plain creepy!'

'I've got a good mind to ground you for the rest of

the holidays,' said Carl. 'In fact…No complaints. You're grounded.'

Mum looked a little puzzled. (I know for a fact she's not the type of parent who thinks grounding is an effective punishment.) But Carl had just gone ahead and done it, and I could tell she was going to agree with him because, apart from her attitude towards Crocs, Mum agrees with Carl on just about everything.

'The thing is, Mum,' I said, 'we really didn't think we'd be bothering anyone. I mean, you guys had the whole house to propose in but you went and did it right in front of—'

'That's not the point, Sunny. I'm sorry, but you're grounded.'

'Please!' said Saskia. 'We didn't spy for long, honest. We stopped as soon as we saw you kiss—'

'That's enough from you, miss!' scolded Carl. 'Now, get to bed, all of you.'

'You can say goodbye to that surveillance thing too, Lyall,' she said. 'Pass it over please.'

'Sorry, Alex,' said Lyall, handing her the monitor.

'I'm sorry too,' said Saskia. 'Even though it was Lyall's idea to spy as well as his idea to steal Ritchie's Crocs.'

I made a dash for the door and ran up to the turret before Lyall went nuts. Unfortunately, Mum followed me up there.

'Mum, I had no idea Lyall would take the shoes. Honest!'

'That doesn't change the fact that you knew he *did* do it. You could have stopped Carl wearing Ritchie's stolen shoes *right in front of him*!' Mum was getting more and more annoyed the more she went on about it. It was time I really put her in her place.

'I'm sorry, Mum, but I had a lot on my mind. I've been dead worried about Flora, for a start. And nobody seems to care about how sad I sometimes feel about Granny Carmelene going off and dying. And that's not even mentioning the fact that I've been experiencing supernatural occurrences that nobody else believes in. And meanwhile, I think it's pretty much official that I've got a crush on a boy who only communicates by writing letters, right when I discover my mother is getting married again when she always told me she wouldn't.

'So, I'm sorry, Mum, for not keeping more of an eye on some ratfink sort-of stepbrother who I didn't even ask to live with in the first place. You dig, Mum? I'm sorry!'

'Enough, Sunny. You're becoming hysterical,' said Mum. 'Now go to bed.' She made her way towards the door.

'Am I really grounded for the rest of the holidays?'

'I'm afraid so. Now get some rest.'

But I couldn't rest because I was thinking too hard. Being grounded was hardly punishment at all. I was going to have to completely fake that I was bothered by it in the slightest. I mean, firstly, most of my friends were away for the holidays. Secondly, I could still have friends *over*, like Finn for instance. Thirdly, Boredom Control was still on, because technically the whole business took place at home. And last but not least, Flora was coming, so I'd been planning on staying around the house for the rest of the school holidays anyway. Yep, being grounded was possibly the best non-punishment in town.

The only thing I had to worry about was finding a cure for Steph's depression and working out how to communicate with the spirit of Granny Carmelene so I could find out exactly where *nowhere* was, once and for all.

24.

It was my favourite kind of cold day – crispy, sunny and not a breath of wind to blow anyone else's dark clouds my way. I had to run an errand for Settimio (even though I was grounded), but Mum said she'd come with me to make sure I didn't do anything wrong.

I was still spying on Settimio, even though I'd promised myself I wouldn't. It was starting to look like an addiction. I just couldn't quit the habit. Still, it wasn't as if he was ever doing anything out of the ordinary – just reading the paper, or making coffee. Surely I'd get bored of spying sooner or later.

On the way to the shops I had two extra springs in my step. One foot had an extra spring on account of Dad, Steph and Flora moving in. And the other was extra springy because Finn was coming over.

I had to play it down though, because it was important that Mum believed I was at least suffering a little bit due to being grounded.

We were waiting at the lights to cross the road to the supermarket when Willow started wagging her tail frantically and pulling on her lead because she saw another dog tied up outside. I could see from a distance that it was Sophia. And with her own collar back on too.

'Calm down, Willow!' I said, as the lights turned green. She was so excited her whole body wanted to break into a few Washing Machines, right in the middle of the intersection. She pulled me hard to where Sophia was tied up, and jumped and pounced all over her.

I was still trying to untangle them when Kara Bleakly appeared with two plastic bags full of shopping.

'Oh, Sunny, it's you,' she said, trying to untie Sophia with one hand while dodging a lick on the face from Willow.

'Hi, Kara,' I said, holding Willow by the collar. 'This is my mum, Alex.' Then I turned to Mum. 'Mum, this is Kara Bleakly.'

'Hello, Kara. Sunny's told us all about you.' Mum held out a hand, which I think she intended as a handshake, but Kara promptly loaded her up with her shopping bags so that she could deal with Sophia.

'Pleased to meet you, Alex. Sunny's been doing a great job with Sophia. She's already lost some weight.'

Mum handed Kara back her shopping bags.

'I think it's the swimming,' I said. 'Sophia's *really* good at it.'

'Which reminds me, Sunny,' Kara went on. 'There was a mix up with the collars the other day. Sophia had the wrong one on when you dropped her off.'

Mum gave me *the eyebrow*.

'Really? I'm so sorry, Kara. I can—'

'Not to worry, Sunny. Luckily the other collar had a contact number on it, so I called the chap, and we set things straight. He lives just around the corner, it turns out.'

'Yes, Ritchie and Woolfie. They're just on Carmichael Drive.'

'Exactly,' said Kara looking at her watch. 'Gosh, I've got to fly. Working most of the weekend again, I'm afraid. Will you be picking Sophia up again tomorrow?'

'Yep, two o'clock,' I said as she took off towards the crossing.

'Lovely to meet you, Alex,' Kara shouted over her shoulder.

'You too, Kara,' Mum called after her, and, when she was certain Kara was out of earshot, Mum said, 'Well, Sunny, your devious matchmaking scheme looks like it's off to a good start. They've met each other at least.

Swapping the dogs' collars, huh? Inspired!'

And I could tell that even though Mum had to be cross with me for my involvement with the Croc theft, she was also dead proud of me at the same time.

As we clicked open the gate I noticed Finn standing on the front porch – and before I could restrain Willow she had darted out in front of me and raced ahead to greet him.

'Watch out!' I called out to him. 'Willow might spook the pigeons.'

'It's okay, Sunny Hathaway, I've put them out of dog reach.' Finn pointed to one of the work vans parked around the side of the house, and sure enough, there was his crate of birds safely sitting on top.

'Hi, Mrs Aberdeen,' Finn said. 'Can I help you with that?'

'Oh, thank you, Finn,' Mum said, allowing him to pull the shopping buggy up the front steps. 'But please, you can call me Alex.'

'I prefer Mrs Aberdeen if you don't mind, Mrs Aberdeen.'

'Finn's got a thing about using people's full names,' I explained as I propped the wire door open for everyone to get inside.

'Fair enough,' said Mum. 'Now, before you both disappear, Settimio needs his parcel from the pharmacy. Why don't you take Finn down to meet him?'

'Aw, Mum! Can't you do it?' I whined.

But before Mum could answer, Finn said, 'Why don't we all go?' Which was a totally weird thing for a friend to say, if you ask me. But let's face it, Finn is hardly regular.

'That's a great idea,' said Mum.

Settimio was waiting in his kitchen with the front door ajar so he wouldn't have to get up from his seat at the table to let us in.

'Knock knock!' Mum called out before we went inside.

'*Grazie mille*,' he said, as Mum put his parcel down on the table.

'This is Sunny's friend Finn,' Mum said. 'Finn Fletcher-Lomax. Finn, this is Settimio Costa.'

Suddenly Mum had become a surname lover too.

'Hello, Mr Costa,' said Finn, and he shook Settimio's hand.

Mum set about unpacking the groceries and Settimio propped himself up against the open door of the fridge, ready to put things away with his spare hand.

'How did he hurt his leg?' Finn whispered.

'He won't tell,' I whispered back. 'You ask him.'

'*Il latte?*' Settimio said, clicking his fingers at me impatiently. '*Milk*,' he repeated.

'Here it is,' said Mum, grouping all the things together that needed refrigeration. 'Lovely sunny day!' she said. 'Finn's been raising pigeons, haven't you, Finn? Sunny, why don't you take Finn outside and show him the old chook house. It might be suitable for pigeons don't you think, Settimio?'

'Pigeons very nice bird,' Settimio said. 'You go take a look.' He nodded sideways at Finn. Then he sighed and sat back down at the table. 'Coffee?' he asked Mum. 'You get coffee?'

'I'd love one,' said Mum. 'Thank you Settimio. Why not?' And just as Finn and I were leaving I noticed Mum take one of Settimio's books down from the shelf above where he has a whole row of little coloured cups, each hanging on its own hook. The book was called *Erbe Medicinali d'Italia*, which even I knew was an Italian book about medicinal plants.

I showed Finn the way to the old chicken coup, which I must say I found a little scary because it was so overrun with long grass and weeds, which could be the perfect hiding place for a tube with fangs, even if it was winter, when snakes are meant to be hibernating.

'Mad,' said Finn, as we stepped inside the cage. 'If I can keep half my pigeons here, we really will be able to reinstate the pigeon post.' He started tugging on some of the weeds in the open air section and made a big pile in one corner.

'I'll put some straw down and mulch over this whole

area,' he said getting as excited about mulching as Mum and Carl.

'Okay,' I said, helping to pull weeds. 'But what did you think about the seance idea, Finn. Will you participate? I'm sure Granny Carmelene's spirit will talk with us straightaway because she's still here. I can feel her and I'm sure that's why she's been sending me angels. As messengers. To let me know she's around.'

'Of course I'll participate, Sunny Hathaway,' Finn said, taking off his pinstriped jacket. 'But how exactly do you talk to spirits? I couldn't find *anything* in our *World Books* or the *Encyclopaedia Britannica*.'

'Oh that part's easy if you have the internet. Leave it to me. The difficult part will be convincing Lyall and Saskia. You see, Saskia gets easily freaked and Lyall's a big fat sceptic.'

Finn used some of the weeds he'd pulled out to sweep out the wooden pigeon holes. 'I hope you won't mind helping look after the birds, Sunny Hathaway? And are you sure it's okay with your Mum?'

Mum and Settimio were still drinking coffee and looking through Settimio's book when we trooped back into the kitchen.

'Where I come from,' said Settimio, stirring two teaspoons of sugar into his coffee, 'the plant you need for medicine is the one that grows right in front of your nose.'

'Yes, I'm familiar with that philosophy,' said Mum. 'Dandelion, for instance; wonderful for the liver, yet most people think it's a weed.'

'Ah *sì, il dente di leone*. Is very bitter plant.'

'It's a beautiful book, Settimio,' Mum said, closing the cover and brushing the dust off with the back of her hand.

'*Sì*, it belong to my grandmother,' said Settimio, throwing back his coffee in one go.

And then I had one of those lightening-bolt light-globe moments when an idea appears and it's just the thing you've been looking for. If it were true that the very thing we need as medicine was the very thing that grows around us in most abundance, then surely at Windermere that plant would have to be roses. Maybe I could make a batch of rose-petal medicine to cure Steph!

After Finn cleared the whole pigeon-keeping arrangement with Mum (Settimio also seemed extremely enthusiastic about helping), he set about explaining the whole pigeon-post concept to me.

'I'm going to let three pigeons fly back to my place and leave the other three here. You'll have to keep them in the enclosure for a good six weeks, because that's how long it will take for their homing mechanism to readjust,' he explained.

'Right on,' I said. 'Sounds simple enough. Food, water, six weeks …'

'Yeah, then, we'll swap your three for my three. The ones that have been at my place will always return to me, and the ones that have been here will fly home to you. Then we just need to find a method for attaching messages. Get it?'

'Kind of,' I said. It all seemed a little complicated, but who was I to argue? I mean if the guy was going to be kind enough to participate in a seance, the least I could do was help him get the pigeon post off the ground.

Once the enclosure was all set up, Finn chose the three birds that would stay at Windermere and put them out in the coop. Then he let the other three go and flapped his arms around so that they wouldn't hang about.

'I guess I'd better get going too, Sunny,' he said, closing the clasps on the empty crate. 'You going to walk me to the bus stop?'

I suddenly felt a little awkward because *everyone* knows that when a boy says *Are you going to walk me to the bus stop?* that he's planning on doing something cringeable like try to kiss you. And, well, it's not that I wasn't prepared to give kissing a try, it was more that I didn't really want my first kiss to be a part of some boy's *Are you going to walk me to the bus stop?* master plan. Even if it was Finn. I'd be worried about it the whole way, which would spoil everything.

My plan was that there would be no plan at all, as far as

you can plan to not have a plan, if you know what I mean.

'Gee, Finn, 'I said. 'I really would like to but I'm kind of grounded.' And right at that moment Dad's car pulled up. 'It's them! It's them!' I shouted, clapping my hands and running as fast as I could to open the front gates so that Dad could drive the car in.

Finn followed me and I introduced him quickly to Dad and Steph through the car window, before Dad continued up the drive.

'So, next time,' I said as I closed the gate with Finn on the other side of it, 'the seance?'

'Sure thing, Sunny Hathaway,' he said. 'Keep an eye on those birds now, won't you?'

I don't know if it was my imagination, but to me Steph looked better already. Maybe it was just because she'd made an effort to get out of her sloppy tracksuit pants. Dad was busy getting all the baby equipment out of the car and Flora was fast asleep in her capsule thing.

'Come inside, Steph,' said Mum, putting an arm around her. 'I've got the kettle on.'

'Sunny!' called Dad. 'How 'bout you take the portacot upstairs?' He handed me a rectangular bag with a handle.

'Dad, did you hear Mum and Carl are getting married? We're having a big feast right here in the spring and I'm going to be a flower girl, and can Flora come, Dad? Pleeease?'

'Let's just get set up here first, Sunny. One thing at a time.'

Dad and I lugged everything upstairs (including Flora, still asleep in her capsule), making sure Willow didn't sneak into anyone's bag and steal a toothbrush to chew on. When everything was up in Granny Carmelene's old room I ran down to the kitchen to find Steph, because I wanted to be the one to show her to the guest room

'Tada!' I said, as I swept open the door. Mum had even lit a scented candle to make it smell nice.

'My goodness,' said Steph, 'What a beautiful room. I really don't feel like I deserve it.' She looked over to Dad, all tearily.

'You *do* deserve it Steph. And you can stay as long as you like,' I said, wishing like anything that Flora could stay forever.

25.

That night I went to bed with an unusual feeling of absolute and undeniable *completion*. Kind of like how a homing pigeon must feel when it's been flapping and flapping and finally drops down from the sky when it sees its own rooftop.

All my family was in the one house. I didn't have anywhere else that I belonged, or anyone at all that I was missing.

Except Granny Carmelene, of course. But that would ease up as soon as I'd had the seance and worked out exactly where *nowhere* was. After that I could even sack Bruce and Terry.

I drifted to sleep, knowing that Flora was under the same roof, and so was Dad and so was Mum (even if they were divorced). Even knowing Lyall and Saskia and Carl were there was comforting, and that's saying something.

I woke up with Willow licking my face – right when I was in the middle of a dream.

'How did *you* get in?' I said, turning away and pulling the covers over my face. Willow jumped up on top of me and started digging at the blankets as if she was trying to find a buried bone.

'Off, Willow!' I squealed, trying to sit up. She leapt down and stood by the door, wagging her tail and smiling.

'Okay, I'm up. Are you happy now?'

She barked, as if to say, *Sure am.*

I looked out the window. There was the thickest fog that made the whole garden look all Peter Rabbity, and I caught a glimpse of Settimio in the orchard, but there was no way I was going to be able to see anything through the telescope because the visibility was so poor. Besides, I knew what he was up to anyway. Mum was taking him to the doctor to get his plaster off. (He hadn't even told *her* how come he'd needed it in the first place.)

I put on my ugg boots and dressing gown and ran down the turret stairs. The door to the guest room was closed tight, which meant Steph and Flora were probably still asleep. I could hear Dad's voice down in the kitchen.

Saskia's door was closed too, so I gave a gentle knock and poked my head inside.

'Pssst, want to help me make something later?' She didn't actually answer but just gave a kind of moan, which I took as a yes.

Willow was still at the top of the turret stairs and gave a whimper.

'I'm *not* carrying you, Willow!' I said, and she must have known I was serious because she trotted straight down onto the landing and then down the next flight too, all by herself.

Carl was busy tossing something in a frypan, and Mum was at the table with her head buried in the crossword, one hand on a coffee cup and the other clutched around a biro.

'Ah, morning, Sunny,' said Dad, looking up from the business section of the paper.

'Hi, Dad,' I said. 'Did Flora sleep okay?'

'She was a *little* unsettled, but nothing too far out of the ordinary for a baby her age.'

'What's cooking, Carl?' I asked, not quite sure if it smelt good or not.

'Not bacon,' said Carl, 'with mushrooms.'

I was a little confused. 'If it's *not* bacon, then what is it?'

'It's *Not Bacon*, that's what it's called,' said Carl, showing me the packet. 'Baconless bacon. It's made out of bean curd. It's delicious, Sunny. It tastes just like bacon.'

Saskia appeared at the kitchen door rubbing the sleep out of her eyes.

'Morning,' she said. 'Yum, bacon.'

'It's Not Bacon, actually,' I said, 'but the good news is it tastes just like bacon.' I held up the packet.

'So it's *fake* bacon? Why don't they just call it Faken?' asked Saskia.

Carl laughed out loud. 'That's funny. Why didn't I think of that? Do you want some Faken, Saskia?'

'Nah, thanks, Dad. I think I'll have cereal.'

'Well, got to fly,' said my dad, putting his bowl in the dishwasher. He leant over and gave me a kiss. 'You help look after Steph now, won't you, Sunny? I've got a bit of running around to do this morning, then I'll come back and say goodbye and get a cab to the airport.'

'Okay,' I said. 'I was thinking Steph might even like breakfast in bed. It would be like room service.'

'Perhaps not Not Bacon,' said Dad, winking at Carl before he left.

'Dad, don't tell me you're turning vegetarian,' said Saskia with her mouth full of cereal.

'Okay, I won't tell you I'm turning vegetarian,' said Carl. 'Faken, Alex?'

'Sorry?' said Mum, looking up from the crossword as

if she'd just dropped in from another planet. 'This DA person is impossible. I've only got about three out. What did you say, Carl?'

'Does that mean you *are* turning vegetarian?' said Saskia.

'Not necessarily,' said Carl.

'Because if *we* have to go vegetarian, I'm going to go live at Mum's.'

Saskia and I made breakfast for Steph and carried it upstairs on a tray. I could hear Flora making gurgling noises, so I knew Steph was awake. Saskia held the breakfast tray while I knocked on the door.

'Come in,' said Steph softly.

'Room service,' I said gently opening the door. 'We brought you some brekkie.'

'You're a doll, Sunny,' said Steph. She was propped up in bed breastfeeding Flora, so I put the tray on her bedside dresser and noticed Saskia had slunk back downstairs, closing the door behind her.

'Has your dad already gone?' she asked.

'A little while ago. But he's coming back before going to the airport. Didn't he say goodbye?'

Steph shook her head. 'It's okay,' she said tearily. 'He probably thought we were asleep and didn't want to wake us. I hope all this isn't putting you off, Sunny – off having babies, I mean,' said Steph.

'Not at all. Anyway, Steph, you're really lucky because not only have I seen an angel in this very room, but Saskia and I are going to make you some medicine that I'm practically certain will cure your PND. Want to go for a walk later? I'll show you and Flora around the garden.'

'Sure,' said Steph. 'As long as you're not in any sort of a hurry.'

I ran back downstairs to find Saskia. She was in the drawing room arguing with Lyall about who was going to tell the Archers that Banjo should be expelled from Boredom Control.

'You should tell them, Lyall; you're the boss, and everyone knows that bosses are the ones who do the sacking.'

'She's got a point, Lyall,' I said. 'I mean, you're not the boss of *me*, but you are the boss of Boredom Control. It was all your idea.'

'But I'm not the one who wants to sack him,' said Lyall. 'You guys do, so it's your job to tell the Archers.'

Saskia grumbled and stomped out of the room.

'Hey, Saskia,' I said following her towards the back door. 'Do you know what?'

'What?' said Saskia.

'If we do decide Banjo has to go, we can always just call them up. With any luck we'll get the answering machine'

'Thanks, Sunny, but maybe we should give Banjo one last chance. I mean, I'm meant to pick him up later today.

It's not really fair to sack him without warning.'

'Come on, help me collect some rose petals then. I'm making a special medicine for Steph.'

'Okay, if you think it will help.'

Saskia and I got an old ceramic bowl from the pantry and went outside. 'We have to put some water in the bottom. We'll use some from the rainwater tank,' I said.

'How do you know how to make medicine anyway, Sunny?'

'I read about it in one of Mum's books about flower essences, but I got the idea to use rose petals from Settimio's book and a conversation he was having with Mum.'

'But what does a *flower essence* actually do?'

'They're used for emotional things and they heal with vibration so subtle that you can't really feel it, but your soul can, if you know what I mean.' I put a small amount of water in the bottom of the bowl.

'Would there be anything a person could take to make them get dyslexia, do you think?' said Saskia, watching how I carefully pulled a couple of petals from each rose and floated them in the bowl of water.

'I don't think so, Saskia, but there might be a flower-essence remedy for a person who is *obsessed* with wanting to be dyslexic when clearly they're not.'

'Sunny, if you were *really* serious about being an artist, you'd want dyslexia too.'

'Saskia, you can still be a great artist or a great *anything* and *not* be dyslexic. It's not a prerequisite.'

'Yeah, but if there was something I could take just before Dad gets me tested …' I mean, I've memorised most of the warning signs and symptoms, but it would be great to have some help.'

'Saskia! You can't *fake* the test. What's wrong with you?'

'Nothing … unfortunately. I'm just so – so – *normal*. It's unbearable!'

'Oh no, you're not,' I said under my breath.

And Saskia said, 'Pardon?'

And I said, 'How would you feel about trying to communicate with the spirit of Granny Carmelene. Finn said he'd join in next time he comes over.'

'I hardly even know Finn.'

'You'll really like him, Saskia. He's *not* normal.' I thought Saskia would be too scared to be a part of a seance, but the idea of it really seemed to cheer her up. For the rest of the petal-collecting time she was quiet and focussed, which is exactly how you're meant to be while making a flower-essence remedy, according to Mum's book, kind of like you're meditating. It's all about concentrating really hard on how you hope the medicine will work, kind of like the visualisation techniques that Auntie Guff taught me.

Don't ask me why, but while I was picking rose petals, I

daydreamed about Steph sitting at a long table with Flora asleep in her arms … There is a crisp white tablecloth and posh crystal glasses and loads of friends and family around. Settimio is even there too. And Steph is just like the old Steph, laughing and chatting and making goo-goo eyes over Flora. And then she's laughing at some kind of joke and I'm thinking that perhaps it's a joke *I* told her, and Steph is laughing and laughing, so hard that when Lyall and Saskia ask her what she's finding so funny, she can't even answer them because she's laughing so hard … and that's where the daydream ends.

'What now?' said Saskia, holding the bowlful of petals.

'Now we leave it to sit in the sun for a couple of hours and then we leave it out for the night to soak up the moon.'

Saskia looked up to the wintry sky. 'Hardly any sun at all today,' she said.

'I know, I know,' I said. 'But that's just from our perspective. As far as the sun's concerned it's beaming away like it always does. Just over the other side of the clouds.'

26.

I was hoping that by the time I got back Steph would be ready for a walk, but the guest room door was shut tight and Dad had told me not to knock or disturb her, on account of depressed people needing a lot more sleep than regular people.

'Hey, Sunny,' called Lyall from the library as I came downstairs. 'There's a letter for you. Looks like it's from your *boyfriend*.'

'Grow up, Lyall.' I almost punched his arm but chose instead to grab the envelope. 'He's not my boyfriend.'

The letter was from Finn all right. Not only was he the only person who wrote me letters, but it was in one of his handmade and recycled envelopes. I carefully unstuck the back and found a message written on a smallish card.

NFSH,

Hey there,

About that seance. Do they work during the day? I was thinking I could come over on Saturday, around ten. It's a pity you're grounded because I really want you to come to my house one day too. I'm working on a knitted wall, because Mum found an old knitting machine and it works a treat. I think you'd like my mum too. See you Saturday.

P.S. In a few weeks, you'll be able to send me a reply by pigeon and it will only take a few hours. Mad!

NFFFL x

'Why doesn't your *boyfriend* just, like, use the phone?' said Lyall, as I put the card back in the envelope.

'Probably because *you and your sister* are, like, *always* on it. Have you ever thought of that, Lyall? Besides, soon we're going to be communicating exclusively by pigeon.'

'Yeah, well, have you seen how much Settimio's been feeding those birds? It'll be a wonder if they can fly at all. There're starting to look more like penguins. You'd better say something to him, Sunny. Really.'

'Really?' I said.

'Really,' said Lyall.

'Hey, Lyall,' yelled Saskia bursting through the back door. 'Where are you?'

'We're in here!' Lyall shouted back at her.

'Shhh, you guys. Flora's asleep!' I said as Saskia found us in the library.

'I've made some jumps,' she said, still puffing. 'For the dogs this afternoon. Come and see, you guys.'

'They're not horses, Saskia,' said Lyall. 'How are we meant to get dogs to go over jumps?'

'With treats, Lyall. Like how you make a dog do anything else,' said Saskia.

Willow looked up at me as if to say, *It's true, treats work. You should really try them more often.*

Saskia had made a whole circuit of jumps down on the flat part near the river. There were eight of them in total, made out of wooden garden stakes, propped up on whatever she could find.

'Look, I'll show you. Come on, Willow, follow me!' Saskia started running and took the first jump, checking behind her to see if Willow was following, which ... she wasn't.

'Come on, Willow!' Saskia stood on the other side of the first jump and reached down deep into her pocket. Willow, clearly suspecting a treat, pricked up her ears and ran over to her, and Saskia took the next jump with Willow close behind, and then the next one, hoping Willow would catch on. Willow didn't exactly *jump*, though. She spent a few moments sniffing the garden stake, and, with Saskia desperately coaxing from the other side, eventually stepped over it, as though it was a puddle that wasn't worth lying down in.

'Good girl!' said Saskia feeding her a leathery doggie treat. 'She's getting the idea! Come on, Willow, next one!'

Saskia started running again, with Willow pacing directly beside her, licking and nibbling at her hand rather than watching *at all* where she was going.

'Jump, Willow!' commanded Saskia as she hurdled the next jump.

Willow, of course, ran straight through it, knocking the stake over as well as the two buckets that were supporting it. She got such a fright that she yelped and ran away, as if she thought perhaps the jump was going to chase her. Then she suddenly became self-conscious, probably because Lyall and I were laughing so much, so she hurried towards me and buried her head between my knees.

'Don't be embarrassed, Willow,' I said, stroking her head. 'Lyall, stop laughing; you'll hurt her feelings.'

'Well,' said Saskia. 'Maybe it would work better if she was on her leash?'

'Maybe it would work better if she was a horse!' mocked Lyall. 'The only ones who'll be getting a workout are us!'

'I don't care!' said Saskia, running toward the front gate. 'I gotta go get Banjo. He'll jump. I just know it!'

Lyall and I were on our way to picking up Woolfie and Sophia when I remembered Ritchie's Crocs.

'I forgot,' said Lyall. 'I'll have to put them back next time. Don't worry, Ritchie will never know it was us.'

'You mean, Ritchie will never know it was *you*,' I said.

'Have it your way, Sunny,' sighed Lyall. 'Come to Ritchie's with me anyway, and pick up Woolfie.'

'Only if you agree to have a seance with me and Finn. So that we can commune with the spirit of Granny Carmelene.'

'What about, Saskia?'

'She's in. She can hardly wait.'

Lyall looked at me suspiciously.

'Come on, Lyall, what else are kids meant to do when they're grounded?'

'Okay,' Lyall said. 'But if the whole thing backfires I'm not taking the blame.'

When we got to Ritchie's, Lyall and I were greeted by the most unexpected surprise. Sophia was running about in Ritchie's front garden with Woolfie.

Lyall and I looked at one another in amazement, right at the exact moment the front door opened, and Ritchie and Kara appeared on the verandah … *together!*

'Well, thanks a million, Ritchie,' said Kara, just before they noticed us. 'Oh, Sunny,' said Kara awkwardly. 'We meet again. And hello, Lionel. Sorry, was it Lionel?'

'Lyall,' we answered at the same time.

'I'm so sorry, Lyall,' Kara said, burrowing through her bag for her keys.

'Come on in, guys,' said Ritchie holding Sophia by the collar, as if he'd known her all his life. 'Kara and I were just chatting about her leaving Sophia here from time to time, for play days. Since she and Woolfie seem to have become such great friends and all – thanks to the wonderful team at Boredom Control.'

Kara laughed. It was kind of like a grown-up version of the fake laugh Claud had developed when she got a crush on Buster.

'Sounds like a great idea,' I said, looking to Lyall.

'Great idea,' he agreed. 'Can't believe we didn't think of it ourselves.'

Kara and Ritchie shot each other a look. Kind of like the one Mum and Carl exchanged when they realised Carl was wearing Ritchie's stolen Crocs. Then Kara did an about-turn and raced towards the gate.

'Okay then, I'll be off,' she said. 'Maybe after you've finished your routine you could drop Sophia back here? At least then she'll have some company for the rest of the day. I've got to work late again.'

'Sure,' I said, clipping on Sophia's leash as Kara squeezed out the gate.

'No stress, Kara,' said Ritchie. 'Pick her up whenever

you like.' He watched her get in her car and waved her off.

'Nice lady,' said Lyall.

'You betcha,' Ritchie smiled.

'Sorry about that mix up with the collars,' I added. 'It won't happen again.'

'Fine by me, kiddo, you can give me an excuse to call Kara any old time you like.'

As you may have guessed, the jumps weren't exactly a huge success, but I didn't want to be the sort of person who says *I told you so*, so I tried my hardest to help Saskia make them work. Besides, I really wanted to be in a position where Saskia owed me a little generosity, as she'd be sure to freak out when seance time actually did come around. (I must say, Willow didn't exactly help matters. She kept distracting the other dogs in an attempt to get one or all of them to chase her around the house.)

'Forget it!' Saskia shrieked eventually, stamping her foot.

'Let them run for a while,' I said, hanging the leashes on the wooden railing at the back verandah stairs. 'They *are* meant to be losing weight after all.'

Just as I opened my mouth to comment on Banjo's exemplary behaviour, he suddenly stopped speeding about with the others and began barking at them instead.

'Oh no,' I said. 'Banjo's got that look again. Like he's seeing the world through *round-'em-up* coloured glasses.'

He crouched down on all fours, trying to look as if he was invisible, obviously planning a pounce.

'Banjo, *stay!*' I said, holding up my hand like a stop sign. But it was too late. Banjo lurched out at Willow, who was the first to pass him, and crunched his jaws around her back foot.

Willow gave a yelp I'd never heard before. Then she growled and gnashed her teeth at Banjo, and ran over to cower behind my legs. She was holding one of her back feet up off the ground, and I could see a puncture wound and blood.

'Oh no!' I wailed. '*He's done it again!*'

'Oh my!' cried Saskia, pointing towards the other dogs. They were piled up on top of one another in one big angry doggie brawl. 'Dog fight! Lyall, do something!'

It was a dog fight all right. A growling tumble-dryer of teeth and claws, and it seemed to be getting more and more intense.

'Daaaaaaaaad!!' screamed Saskia.

'Dad's not here, idiot!' yelled Lyall.

Willow was shaking, but I didn't want to move in case Banjo shifted his focus from savaging Woolfie and Sophia and tried to take on me and Willow instead.

That's when Steph appeared at the back door in her nightie. *Steph* of all people, and she looked dead angry too. She stomped down the back steps and snatched the hose up from where it was lying by the herb garden.

'I know there are water restrictions and all, Lyall, but turn it on full blast, would you? *Hurry!*' yelled Steph.

Lyall did exactly as he was told, reassuring Steph that the hose was from the greywater tank we used for the garden, so we weren't wasting good drinking water.

Steph set the hose on the dog fight, focusing on squirting Banjo. The three of them separated at once and whenever one even looked like moving she blasted them with water.

'Now, put their leashes on!' she yelled. 'And tie them up well away from one another.'

Lyall and Saskia set to it while Steph turned the hose off and came over to inspect Willow's foot. The skin was broken, but it wasn't very deep. Banjo had pretty much given Willow the same wound as he'd given me. 'Should be okay,' said Steph. 'Just give it a wash, Sunny.'

'I will,' I said. 'Sorry to disturb you, Steph. Thanks for breaking up the fight.'

'Don't mention it,' said Steph. 'It seems like that dog doesn't need Boredom Control. He'd do better with some Anger Management.' Then she became suddenly self-conscious, as if she'd only just realised she was walking around in her nightie. 'I'd better go check on Flora,' she said.

I carried Willow up the back steps, and set her down

on the doormat, where she curled herself over and began sorrowfully licking her bitten foot.

'I'm sorry, girl,' I said gently patting her head. 'In your own home too; that's just rude!'

I looked over to where Lyall had tied Banjo to the pipes on the wall near the tap. Banjo looked every bit pleased with himself, as if he'd do it all again in a flash if he had half a chance.

It was lucky for us (and for them!) that neither Sophia nor Woolfie were hurt in the dog fight, but can you believe Lyall *still* wanted to give Banjo another chance?

'Not on your life, Lyall!' I said as we were drying Woolfie and Sophia off.

'Forget it, Lyall,' Saskia added. 'We already agreed that *today* was his last chance and that sacking him was going to be *your* job.'

'Fine,' said Lyall. 'I'll sack him if he plays up next time.'

'No way!' I said. 'I'm taking him straight back to the Archers' right now and sacking him myself. You coming, Saskia?'

'Absolutely,' confirmed Saskia. 'That dog is *out*, Lyall, and there's nothing you can do about it.'

It was only as Saskia and I were marching Banjo back to his home that I realised Lyall had used Reverse Psychology on me.

'That sneaky little …'

'What?' asked Saskia.

'Have a look at us. Lyall got what he wanted, didn't he?'

'But he wanted Banjo to stay,' said Saskia.

'No, silly, what he really wanted was to drop Banjo, but not to have to do it himself. He just *pretended* he wanted Banjo to stay so he wouldn't have to do the sacking part.'

'Ugh! That's so typical Lyall.'

Banjo pulled on his leash as we approached the Archer's front fence and started wagging his tail like crazy when he saw Mr Archer collecting the mail.'

'Hi, girls!' he said. 'How was Boredom Control today?'

It wasn't easy giving Banjo the sack, I can tell you. Still, it had to be done and in the end I had to do it all. Saskia just stood there and acted as if she didn't speak English.

Mr Archer assured us Banjo had absolutely *never* bitten anyone before, especially not other dogs. Eventually I got Mr Archer to understand that we didn't think Banjo was the right sort of customer for Boredom Control. I mean, we were fine with him on the issue of relieving *boredom* but were absolute failures when it came to *control*. In the end I just showed him my ankle, which was still bruised. That made all the difference.

Saskia and I walked most of the way home in silence.

'Are you cross with me, Sunny?' she asked sheepishly, knowing she shouldn't have dumped the whole job on me.

But I wasn't really that annoyed with Saskia. She is

only nine after all. Mostly I was annoyed with myself for not detecting Lyall's implementation of payback Reverse Psychology. Reverse-Reverse Psychology – who would have thought?

27.

It was getting dark when I knocked gently on Steph's door.

'Come in,' I heard her say, so I eased the door open and shut it quietly behind me.

She was in bed reading, and Flora was next to her, fast asleep with her arms up above her head as if she was floating.

'Hi, Sunny,' she said. 'Flora's been asleep for hours, so I thought I'd make the most of it and have a bath and a read. Sorry about our walk. The day just seemed to slip away.'

'That's okay.'

'It really is lovely up here. It's like another world. I'm not going to want to go home – kind of dreading it actually, even if we are flush with freezer meals.'

'I don't want you to go home either,' I said. Even thinking about it made me get throat ache.

'Mum and Carl said that we can bring dinner up to you later, like a real hotel or a hospit—'I suddenly thought that I shouldn't mention hospital, considering that there had been talk of Steph having to go there.

'You know what, Sunny? I know you're not meant to *enjoy* a dog fight, but there was something about hosing that crazy dog away that gave me a big surge of energy. I feel like I've got a bit of life in me again. Strange, isn't it?'

'Wow,' I said. 'Maybe Banjo wasn't such a disaster after all.'

Flora made a few stirring noises and opened her eyes.

'Can I have a hold?' Steph nodded and I slid my hand gently under Flora's head and scooped her off the bed and into my arms. 'There you go, Flora,' I said. 'It's me again, your naughty big sister, Sunny.'

Flora studied my face for the longest time, because when you're that young you can stare at people without anybody telling you that it's bad manners. I could also see her looking about for Steph. 'Mumsy's right here, Flora, no need to worry.'

Flora looked at me again as if to wonder whether I was a reliable source. I guess she thought I was, because her whole face broke into the biggest smile ever. Then she looked dead serious again, as though perhaps she was worried for me about the goo-goo baby noises I was making as I smiled back at her.

'Yes Flora,' I said. 'You're going to love it here, yes you are, yes you are, yes you are.'

I got to hold Flora all through dinner because she cried every time we put her in the pram. Then Saskia had a turn while I ate my fish.

'Would you like a hold too, Lyall?' Steph asked,

'Oh, no thanks, maybe later,' said Lyall. 'I like babies but, like, babies don't really like me. I'm kind of better with cats and dogs.'

'Ooooh yeah, Lyall's *reeeeeally* good with dogs. Yes siree,' said Saskia, knowing that she was safe from getting a punch from Lyall while she was holding a baby.

'That reminds me, Lyall,' said Carl. 'You did return Ritchie's Crocs today didn't you?'

'Kind of,' answered Lyall.

'*Kind of!* It was a simple question Lyall. You either put them back or you didn't. Now, which is it?'

'We need this whole thing resolved by Saturday,' Mum said. 'Ritchie's coming to the working bee. Oh, and Kara called to say she was coming too, which is great.'

'Kara doesn't even *like* gardening,' I said, before I remembered how sometimes people *pretend* to like things when they're trying to impress someone. '

Steph was looking as if she'd missed a couple of key episodes of her favourite soap opera.

'Sorry, Steph,' said Mum. 'We're expanding the vegetable garden to include community plots, and our action group is coming on Saturday to implement Stage One.'

'What a great idea,' said Steph.

'Thanks,' continued Carl. 'Our ultimate goal is eventually to have zero carbon emissions. The solar's underway, and we've got room for a small wind turbine too.'

'Anyway, enough about us. How did things go for you today, Steph?' asked Mum.

'I was perfectly spoilt and even got an afternoon nap,' said Steph, not even mentioning the dog fight.

28.

By eight-thirty on Saturday morning the people from Mum and Carls' action group had started to arrive. From up in my turret room I could see everything going on. Carl had pegged out a whole area of lawn that had to be mulched over and turned into vegetable plots, and there was lots of wood and stakes and piles of soil to start making raised garden beds. Kara was blowing into her hands to warm them up. She was wearing the most inappropriate pair of wedge-heeled trainers you've ever seen at a working bee. I saw Mum saying something to her, and because I can often tell the sort of things that go on in Mum's head, I'm sure she was saying something like, *If you want to borrow some gumboots, Kara, we may be about the same size.* And then I imagined Ritchie thinking that Kara Bleakly might be the perfect candidate for a pair of Crocs. By the end of the day, Ritchie's Crocs would have mysteriously reappeared. Was Kara going to find out the real truth about Ritchie and dump him?

I had to get my bowl of rose petals, so I snuck out the front door to avoid having to answer a whole lot of adult questions about how old I am and whether or not I enjoy school. I mean, why can't adults talk about anything interesting, like where exactly a person goes when they die and whether or not it's possible to communicate with spirits.

When Saskia and Lyall finally came downstairs I had already bottled my flower-essence remedy and was making a tag for it with some stamps I'd got for Christmas.

Lyall poured himself some cereal as if he was on auto pilot. 'I'm so going to be hiding from Dad today,' he crunched. 'Otherwise we'll have to help in the garden.'

'You're meant to *want* to help, Lyall,' said Saskia, buttering her toast, and I'm sure he would have punched her in the arm if he hadn't been still so half asleep.

'Oh, we'll be hiding all right,' I said. 'In the dining room, having a seance. Right after we get back from Ritchie's.'

'What if I actually don't want to join in?' said Saskia, with a mouth full of toast.

'Don't then,' I said, thinking I'd try Reverse Psychology just one last time. 'You can keep watch.'

Woolfie and Sophia must have recognised our voices because by the time we opened Ritchie's gate the two of them were barking their heads off.

'*Shhhhh*, you two,' I said, and instantly the barking-fest turned into a licking-and-tail-wagging-fest as we all squeezed through the gate. 'Saskia, can you grab the leashes,' I said, holding Sophia by her collar. 'They're up on the meter box near the front door.' Woolfie ran after her.

That's when I noticed what Lyall was up to. He had taken Ritchie's green Crocs out of his backpack and was rubbing them in a patch of dirt. I gave him *the eyebrow*.

'It's got to look like they've been buried and dug up again,' said Lyall. Woolfie gave Lyall a suspicious look.

'Sorry, Woolfie,' said Lyall. He put one shoe on the front doormat and left the other one face down, partly buried under Ritchie's lemon tree. 'That should do it,' he said.

'Now we've just got to stop Dad getting a new pair,' said Saskia.

'Or Ritchie buying a pair for Kara,' I added.

'That's okay,' Lyall said. 'I'll just remind Dad and Ritchie that we live in a world dominated by consumerism and that they really shouldn't be adding to it by creating the demand for two more pairs of Crocs.'

'That will *definitely* work on Carl,' I said. 'But I don't know about Ritchie. He does work in *advertising* remember?'

'Can we *go* now?' said Saskia, with a leashed dog in each hand.

When we got back, Willow, Woolfie and Sophia ran about like crazy, as usual, with Willow out in front (her leg didn't look as if it was bothering her in the slightest), and the other two following close behind.

'Hey, can you two watch them a while? I have to check on Finn's pigeons.'

I ran down to the old chook pen behind Settimio's cottage. All three birds were safe, each perched inside a seperate pigeon hole. I saw straight away why dumb old Lyall had thought they looked too fat to fly: they had all their feathers ruffled up against the cold. Settimio had obviously been looking after them well (just like Mum said he would); there was fresh straw in all the pigeon holes for them to snuggle into at night. But I almost jumped out of my skin when I heard his voice behind me.

'Looking good, you think?' he said, peering through the wire.

'Oh, Settimio, you gave me a fright. Hey, you got your plaster off!'

'This one especially looking good.' Settimio pointed to the greyish one with the darker grey stripes on its wings.

'I kind of like the brownish-red one,' I said.

'Blue one better. This one best,' he said. I was surprised that Settimio knew which one was going to be the best homing pigeon just by looking at it, but I went along with it anyway.

'Need to feed them good, and then in a few weeks, they be just perfect. Maybe ready by time is wedding.'

I imagined how wonderful it would be if the pigeons could fly out of a box right when Mum and Carl did their wedding kiss, like I saw once on TV. I'm sure it wouldn't matter at all if Finn's pigeons weren't exactly white doves.

'Great idea, Settimio! Wedding pigeons!'

'Of course,' he said.

After that I ran around to the front door and bounded up the stairs two-by-two to deliver my flower-essence remedy to Steph. Only thing was, neither she nor Flora were anywhere to be seen so I put the small bottle next to Steph's side of the bed and ran back downstairs. Mum was buttering some fruit buns, getting ready for morning tea. 'Where's Steph?' I said, still puffing.

'Outside I think, love. Want to give me a hand here?"

'Soon!' I said making a dash for the back door, almost knocking over Saskia on her way in.

'Mum wants you to help her with morning tea,' I said.

'Sunny Hathaway!' Mum yelled as I was flying down the back steps.'I heard that!'

'Have you seen Steph and Flora?' I asked Carl, looking

236

super-flustered, as if I was on an important mission. That way, he'd be less likely to give me a job. Carl pointed over to Settimio's cottage, and I saw Flora's pram parked right outside. 'How the heck? I was just over there and didn't even see them.'

'It's a wonder you notice *anything*, Sunny, running about like you do. They must have come out the back door right when you went in the front.' Carl had hardly finished his sentence before I made a run for it to Settimio's cottage.

'See if you can encourage Settimio to come and meet the group!' Carl called out after me. 'We'd love for him to get involved!'

Settimio's door was open, but I knocked anyway because that's the good manners thing to do in that sort of situation. I heard a chair scrape against the kitchen floor and when he appeared at the front door would you believe he was holding Flora?

'Oh, hello again, Settimio,' I puffed, feeling suddenly possessive about Flora. 'That's my baby sister, actually, in case you don't know, Settimio.'

'Come in, Sunday, please,' said Settimio, gesturing towards the kitchen with his Flora-free hand.

I could tell Steph had been crying because her eyes were all puffy and red, and she quickly put her sunglasses on – inside.

'You okay?' I asked.

Settimio leant down and passed the sleeping bundle of Flora back to Steph. Then he busied himself making a coffee.

'Up and down,' said Steph. 'It's nice to be out for a walk. I felt wonderful yesterday and then this morning – crash!'

'Oh, Settimio, that reminds me,' I said. 'Carl said he'd love for you to help with the vegetable garden, if you'd like to.'

'Maybe I could be scarecrow?' giggled Settimio, making a scary face and standing with his arms outstretched. Then he started laughing and the best part was it made Steph chuckle too, and I didn't know how long it had been since Steph had had even the tiniest bit of a laugh.

'Hey, Steph,' I said, 'I left you a little present next to your bed. I made it myself, and it's got instructions and everything.'

29.

As soon as Finn had arrived and said hello to Lyall and Saskia, he ran straight down to see the pigeons. We all followed him, trying our best to avoid the action group.

Willow, Sophia and Woolfie bounded along behind us. Willow barked at the pigeon cage a few times, but really just to see if she'd get any attention, which she did.

'No, Willow!' we all said at once, except Finn, who possibly thought it wasn't his place to discipline my dog. (Kind of like how Carl was at the start, before his whole polite act wore off.)

Finn let himself into the pen and closed the door behind him. He moved slowly towards one of the pigeon holes and let his hands descend gently upon the speckledy-red bird.

'Soon we'll have to make some little gates for the cage, so they can let themselves back in when they've flown home. Kind of like a cat door,' he said.

'Did you know I'm dyslexic, Finn?' asked Saskia from the other side of the wire.

Both Lyall and I glared at her, and I could tell Finn didn't really know what to say or even whether to believe Saskia or not. I mean, why couldn't she just say something normal, like, *What year are you doing at school?*

'Should we head back inside now?' I asked, thinking that it was high time we got our seance underway. Especially as absolutely all the adults were safely occupied outside. It was the perfect opportunity.

'Come on, you guys,' I said. 'The dining room.'

So far we hadn't used the dining room once. It had huge wooden doors at one end that opened onto the drawing room and another door where you could enter through the hallway near the kitchen. There was a long table all the way down the middle and windows that looked out to the side verandah, and a part of the ceiling was all slanty where the staircase cut through.

'Wow,' said Finn. 'Is this where you're having the wedding feast?'

'It's Plan B actually,' I said. 'We're hoping the weather will be nice enough to set it up outside.

'Will this be scary?' asked Saskia. 'I don't even know

what you do in a seance anyway.'

'Oh no, it will be fine,' Finn assured her. 'You just ask questions, and if there's a spirit present they answer for you. I found out my mum used to have seances all the time. Once she even spoke to the spirit of Rembrandt. You know, the artist?'

I almost wanted to hug Finn then, because that was *the* perfect answer to give Saskia the reassurance she needed. But I managed to restrain myself in front of the precookeds.

'Rembrandt was dyslexic, wasn't he?' asked Lyall, just to add a little icing to the convincing-Saskia cake.

'Cool!' squealed Saskia. 'How do we start?'

There was an old fireplace at one end of the room and a rug between the hearth and one end of the table.

'I think we should sit here,' I said, standing on the rug. 'But we have to draw all the blinds first and make it dark.'

'I'll do it,' said Lyall, reaching to pull the cord of the nearest one. 'Man, these are stiff. They feel as if they haven't been used in years,' he said as I closed the double doors to the drawing room as well as the door to the hall.

Saskia and Finn were already sitting cross-legged on the rug.

'Don't we need a candle?' said Finn.

'Good point,' I said, and opened the hallway door again to let some light in while I found a candle, a candlestick and some matches in the sideboard where Granny Carmelene kept the good silver cutlery. I put the candlestick down in the middle of the rug and lit the candle before closing the door once more.

'Now,' I said. 'Are we ready? We have to all hold hands.' Even while I was secretly hoping to hold Finn's hand, I was also relieved to be sitting between Lyall and Saskia because holding hands with Finn in front of the precookeds would surely make me feel awkward. So I held Lyall's hand, and Lyall held Finn's hand, and Finn held Saskia's hand, and Saskia held one of my hands too. And the light of the candle closed the wideness of the world out; our little bit extended only as far as its flickering glow.

'We should be filming this,' said Lyall. 'Then we could put it on YouTube.'

'Are you kidding, Lyall? As if Granny Carmelene is going to converse with us if she knows she'll end up on the internet. It's just not dignified for a spirit.'

Finn laughed, and I could tell he agreed with me.

'Can we just start now, please?' said Saskia impatiently.

'Okay, then. So, um we have to be quiet and sit and breathe for a while,' I said, and no one answered me because they were all sitting quietly and breathing.

'Do we have to close our eyes?' whispered Saskia.

'I don't think it matters, I whispered back. 'Maybe you can just watch the flame.'

'Good idea,' whispered Saskia.

'Can you stop talking, Saskia,' whispered Lyall.

'Sorry,' whispered Saskia. Then we were all very quiet again for a really long time.

'Okay.' I cleared my throat as I tried to remember exactly what to say.

'We're trying to communicate with the spirit of Carmelene Aberdeen. If the spirit of Carmelene Aberdeen is present would you please give us a sign.'

Suddenly the candle flame flared upwards and Saskia screamed.

'Shh!' we all went at once.

'This is freaky,' whined Saskia.

'It was nothing,' said Lyall. 'Candles always do that. It was probably just an air bubble in the wax.'

I was suddenly regretting that I'd agreed to have a sceptic in the room. I mean, Lyall was going to have a perfectly reasonable explanation for *everything* and surely the spirit of Granny Carmelene would simply get bored and go away.

'Shhhh,' I said. 'Let's continue.'

We all settled again and became quiet. 'If the spirit of Carmelene Aberdeen is present would you mind giving us *another* sign, and I'm really sorry but could you make it a big one because unfortunately Lyall is a sceptic.'

For a while there was nothing but silence.

Then Finn took over and said, 'Carmelene Aberdeen, I'm sorry never to have met you whilst you were on this earthly plane, but if you are at all present in spirit would you mind tapping or something to let us know you—'

There was a definite sound, like when you knock a ruler against your desk at school, but it was difficult to work out exactly where the noise came from. It tapped three distinct times, then stopped.

'That was a tap all right. Did you hear it, Lyall?' I whispered. 'Is that enough of a sign for you.'

'I want to get out of here,' squeaked Saskia. 'I really do.'

'Hello, Carmelene Aberdeen,' continued Finn. 'Do you mind if we ask you a few questions? You can tap once for yes and twice for no.'

There were two more taps.

'That's a no,' I said.

Then there was one loud tap, meaning yes.

'Now I'm really confused. Granny Carmelene, if that's you—' I was cut off by one loud tap.

'Oh bejeezus!' croaked Lyall, and I could feel his hand go all clammy, but I still kept holding it because on the inside I was freaking out myself.

'Okay then, Granny Carmelene, it's really good you're here. I've been missing you a lot, but kind of sensed that you were around, wherever *around* might be. Can I just ask one thing? This angel business – is that actually you?'

One tap

'Told you!' said Lyall.

'You *did* not! Anyway, we're not here to argue,' I whispered forcefully.

Two solid taps.

'See, Lyall, Granny Carmelene agrees.'

'Hurry up, Sunny,' he said. 'Just ask what you need to ask and then let's go. I said I'd help Dad in the garden.'

'Me too,' whispered Saskia.

I'd suddenly forgotten all the things I wanted to say, just like how I felt when I first met Granny Carmelene in real life and went all shy. Not only that, this tapping thing could only give me yes or no answers and what I *really* wanted to know was a little more involved than that. Like, for instance, where exactly was she?

'Can you hurry please, Sunny,' said Saskia once more.

'Are you still there, Granny Carmelene?'

There was a short silence and we all looked about expectantly.

'She's gone,' whispered Saskia. 'It's probably morning-tea time up in heaven. Let's do something else.' She tried to ease her hand out of mine but was interrupted by the sound of a loud tap and squeezed my hand again as tightly as she could. 'Hurry, Sunny, can you just finish your questions. I really need to pee.'

'Shh, Saskia!' scolded Lyall.

'Okay,' I said. 'Granny, is it true about heaven?'

But she didn't get a chance to respond because suddenly there was a huge bang from right behind me and the middle blind flew up all by itself, flooding the room with light. Saskia screamed and I almost jumped out my skin when I saw that the candle had gone out too, and all that was left of the flame was a thin trail of smoke whisping up to the ceiling.

Saskia ran for the door, still screaming, until Lyall pounced on her from behind and covered her mouth.

'Shoosh, Saskia! Just stop! You'll attract attention.' Lyall was as white as a sheet as well. 'It was just the blind, Saskia. Wasn't it, Sunny? Finn?'

'Probably,' said Finn. 'Don't you think, Sunny?' He moved over to where I was standing near the mantelpiece. 'You okay, Sunny Hathaway?' he asked, rubbing my back.

'I'm *fine*,' I said, hurrying to put the candle and matches away. I was more than a little annoyed that perhaps Finn didn't believe we *were* actually communicating with the spirit of Granny Carmelene. Maybe Finn was a sceptic like Lyall? Maybe after the botched seance, Granny Carmelene wouldn't want to communicate with us again. If only I'd done it on my own! What if I was stuck with unanswered questions about somewhere, nowhere and angels for the rest of my life?

Just then, Saskia screamed again, because just as she

reached for the door its handle started turning by itself.

'What on earth are you kids up to?' Steph asked as she opened the door and came in. 'It sounds like someone's being murdered in here.'

'Oh, sorry, Steph,' I said. 'We were just playing a game, Murder in the Dark actually, and well, Saskia got a little freaked. We've finished now though haven't we?' I put my arm around Saskia for a moment. 'It's okay, Saskia, it's only a silly game.'

Lyall and Finn both nodded furiously.

'Sorry if we disturbed you, Steph,' I said. 'I hope we didn't wake Flora. Come on, Finn,' I said. 'Let's see what's happening outside.'

Lyall and Saskia both took off upstairs. Finn and I, on the other hand, headed straight for the back door.

'Hi, you two!' said Mum. 'Feel like helping?'

Before I could answer, Finn shouted out, 'Sure Mrs Aberdeen!'

Willow appeared at top speed when she heard Finn's voice.

'Hello, girl!' I said. 'Where have you been?'

'She's been on the verandah,' said Mum, pointing to the side of the house. 'Frantically gnawing on a huge bone.'

Mum's words triggered something in my brain. I took off up the back stairs and around to the side verandah, with Willow running right behind me. Sure enough, right outside the dining room windows was a big old doggie bone all chewed on one end. Willow stood over it as though she thought I might take it away from her. Then she squatted down and put a paw on one end of the bone to secure it while she chewed the other. With every move of her head the bone made a knocking sound on the hollow wooden verandah.

Finn appeared beside me and we both stood silently for a moment watching Willow with her clunky bone.

'Are you thinking what I'm thinking, Sunny Hathaway?' asked Finn.

And I said, 'I really do believe I am, Finn Fletcher-Lomax. It wasn't the spirit of Granny Carmelene making the knocking sounds; it was Willow. She was right outside the window the whole time.'

'It sure does look that way, Sunny,' he said, and I could tell he was sensing my disappointment.

Finn and I decided to dodge the working bee for a bit and go for a walk by the river. We sat at the table under the willow tree, right where Granny Carmelene and I had eaten eclairs.

'You know what, Sunny Hathaway?' Finn said. And before I could say, 'What?' he continued, 'No one really knows what happens after you die. Our teacher asked our class once and got twenty-four different answers. And do you know what else?'

'What?' I said.

'They were *all* right. You don't need your grandmother to tell you where nowhere is, or whether angels really exist. It's about having a story for yourself that feels right.'

That night, Saskia insisted on sleeping in my bed, even though I'd explained about Willow and her bone making the ghost noises.

'Sorry, Sunny. I'd sleep with Lyall, but ever since he turned twelve he kind of smells,' said Saskia.

She was standing at my bedroom door in her jarmies hugging her pillow. How could I turn her away?

'It's okay, Saskia.' I said. 'Just as long as you don't wet the bed.'

'As if! But do you mind if we leave the light on?' she said, loosening the sheets at the foot of the bed so she could hop in.

'I'll tell you what, Saskia,' I said, 'How 'bout we leave the lava lamp on. Then at least I can get some sleep.'

To keep Saskia's mind off scary things I started talking about Mum and Carl's wedding She seemed to be more excited about it than anyone, even Mum and Carl, and we finally worked out how we could *both* be flower girls. We even worked out a way to make Willow a flower girl too, and maybe even Sophia, if Kara Bleakly said it was all right for her to come.

'It's almost spring, Sunny, I can feel it in the air,' said Saskia. 'I just can't wait. Then it will be summer and we can jump off the jetty into the river. And then it will be Christmas and then it will be my birthday and then ... 'night, Sunny.'

And then it will be Flora's birthday and then it will be my birthday too, I thought to myself. And I kept on thinking, just like I always do in bed at night. I had lots of thoughts about Granny Carmelene, and the good news was there was nothing about my thoughts that made me feel sad one bit. It was as if all of a sudden I could remember her without putting all my energy into trying to stop remembering. And I thought about what Finn had said, and tried as hard as I could to imagine what *nowhere* was like for me. *Nowhere* was floaty and cloudy, but mostly sunny, and it glowed all purple and warm. Kind of like how my turret room feels with the lava lamp on and I'm all snuggled up in bed.

Finn was right. No one could tell me that my idea of *nowhere* was wrong, and I didn't really need Granny Carmelene to tell me that it was *right*, either. The main thing was that it suddenly felt okay for Granny Carmelene to be there – all tucked up in *nowhere*. It made me stop worrying about her being all right.

I drifted off into the most peaceful slumber. And it felt like the sort of slumber where hours and hours had passed, until ...'

Thud!

Saskia woke up and screamed when she saw the expression on my face. And I screamed too, just because seeing her so scared and screamy made me scared and screamy too, and it was so dark outside all we could see were the reflections of our own selves in the windows.

Then there was a thud against the window again, and Saskia dived under the covers and burrowed up to my end of the bed and clung on to me until it hurt.

'Sunny! What is it? Ly-a-all! Daaaaduh!' she yelled.

I was all frozen and silent and actually tried to scream for Mum but couldn't make any noises. The only thing that came was a hopeless squeak. Then there was another thud, an even louder one, and this time a whole pane of glass broke, and without even meaning to I kind of huddled on top of Saskia and pulled the covers over both our bodies, and we screamed and screamed at the top of our voices and this time my scream actually worked so well I'm sure Dad could have heard us all the way over in China. And nothing could stop me screaming because there was actually *something* in the room! Something thumpy!

Finally I heard someone running up the stairs and then Carl say, 'God Almighty!' and Mum yell, 'Are they all right? Sunny? Saskia?'

Then Carl said, 'Don't come in, Alex! I've got to get it out!' and Saskia and I screamed some more and I could hear the thumping thing thumping, and then I heard a screech.

'Shh, girls,' said Carl, and I heard a flap and a thump and a screech, and then I heard Carl saying, 'Shoo!' and there was a rush of cold air in the room and then it was silent.

Saskia was whimpering and clutching onto my arm. Carl gently peeled back the covers and I heard the door handle squeak again as Mum opened it ever so slightly and said, 'For goodness sake, Carl, what on earth is happening?'

And he said. 'Would you believe it was a bat, darl? Flew clean through a pane of glass.'

After the bat incident I had to vacate my room on account of it not having its full complement of windows any more.

'You can share my room, Sunny. I really don't mind,' said Saskia.

I thought about it seriously. I mean, for Flora's sake the more practice I had at being big sister the better, right? And I kind of had always wanted to have one of those rooms with the line down the middle that the other person wasn't allowed to cross when you had a fight. Especially if I made sure my side of the room was the part that had the door.

'Okay, thanks, Saskia,' I said. 'Maybe I will for now.'

What are you kids going to do about Boredom Control now that school's gone back?' Mum asked at breakfast one morning.

'We're still going to take Woolfie one night a week after school. But since Sophia is having regular play days at his place, neither of them are going to need as much entertaining.'

'Yeah,' I added, 'and Kara said she's going to be working less, and that she and Ritchie are going to try to take both dogs for long walks together.' I checked my watch. 'I gotta go, otherwise I'll miss my bus.'

The best part about being back at school was knowing I'd see Finn on the bus each morning, which was a whole lot easier than writing letters or (don't tell Finn) trying to communicate via pigeon.

The other best bit was that I had solid evidence that Finn was an official boyfriend. It wasn't anything he said. It was simply due to the fact that I knew he missed two buses after school to make sure he caught the one with me on it. What more proof does a girl need?

As the weeks whizzed by, we all got totally used to having Steph and Flora in the house. They became part of the family, especially as Dad's time in China kept being extended. I missed him heaps, but let's face it, the longer he was away, the longer I'd have Flora around.

Steph missed Dad too, even though he rang almost every day, but I didn't think she was looking forward to leaving either. But the weirdest part of all was that, with us kids out of the house all day, Steph and Settimio had kind of become best friends.

Every day she and Flora would visit him and they'd drink small, thick cups of coffee with oodles and poodles of sugar and Settimio would go all goo-goo over Flora. (I knew because I was still in the habit of sneaking up to my turret room after school and spying through Settimio's kitchen window with Granny Carmelene's telescope.)

Before we knew it, winter had wintered and spring had clearly sprung. All the bony trees were covered once more with leaves, and the garden was coming alive with flowers. Not to mention the vegetables galore!

It was just days before the wedding, and Mum and Carl were going even more nuts than usual about doing things to the house, including finally getting new glass in my room.

I was up in the turret because Mum had asked me to vacuum the turret floor one last time after the glass people had fitted the new window. So I had a little bit of a spy on Settimio. I mean, it was really for Steph and Flora's sake because they were spending so much time over there, and

I did promise Dad I'd help take care of them. I pulled the telescope into focus just as Steph was standing up to leave. Settimio gave her a kiss on both cheeks and helped release the brake of Flora's pram. After she had left, he appeared in the kitchen and started looking along his shelf, as if he was trying to find a particular book. Finally, he pulled one down, dusted it off and flipped to the index. Then he opened out the book and laid it on the table.

I readjusted my focus to see what the book was. It was in Italian so I couldn't understand it, but it looked like a recipe book. He was probably using it to make his speciality for Mum and Carl's wedding like he'd said he would.

The recipe was headed *Torta di Piccione* and the rest of the left-hand page was full of words that I couldn't understand. I shifted my focus to the other side of the double-page spread, which was a picture of a grey speckled bird.

Torta di Piccione! Suddenly the words made a whole lot more sense.

Pigeon Pie! Can you believe it? Settimio's speciality was *pigeon pie*!

I ran straight downstairs, hoping to catch Steph as she was coming inside. But she was already in the kitchen with Mum, and Flora was happily breastfeeding away.

'Steph!' I said. 'It's terrible. You have to help!'

'What now, Sunny?' asked Mum. She was up the ladder in the pantry sorting jars of preserves and relishes.

'Settimio's planning on making a pigeon pie for the wedding! That's why he's been taking such an interest in Finn's pigeons. So they can fatten up and be *eaten*!'

'Oh, Sunny, are you sure?' said Steph. 'He mentioned he had an old family recipe, but he never mentioned anything about pigeon pie.'

'Where on earth did you get that idea, Sunny?'

I realised that the *only* way I could help Finn and his pigeons was to 'fess up about my spying. I had no choice. What if he was planning on killing the pigeons straightaway?

'I know, Mum, because I was playing with Granny Carmelene's old telescope and I happened to line it up towards Settimio's kitchen window, and I happened to notice that Settimio had a recipe book on his kitchen table and it happened to be a recipe for pigeon pie. Why else would he be looking at *that* if he wasn't planning on making one?'

Mum stepped down from the bottom rung of the ladder.

'You mean you *spied* on Settimio? In his own home? Please tell me you didn't. I'm still getting over the fact that you kids spied on our wedding proposal.' Mum looked dead angry, and the angrier she got the more it made the two big veins in her neck stand out.

'Please don't tell Carl, Mum. Besides, Lyall and Saskia aren't involved.'

'Sunny Hathaway, I just don't know *what* to do with you.'

'Can't you work it out *after* saving Finn's pigeons? Settimio will never listen to me. Please, Mum? Steph? *Please!*'

'Well,' said Steph, looking to Mum for some sort of approval. 'If it's all right with your mum, I could have a talk with him, I guess? I mean, no one *wants* Finn's pigeons to end up in a pie, Sunny.'

'Of course,' agreed Mum. 'Poor Finn would be devastated. Especially as he's invited to the wedding.'

'Alex, I'll finish feeding Flora, then maybe you could watch her for me while Sunny and I go and set things straight.'

It was right at that moment that Carl got home with Lyall and Saskia. I could hear them squabbling about who was going to be sitting next to who at the wedding table.

'Do we have to invite Uncle Lawrence, Dad?' Lyall said. 'He always gets drunk and falls asleep.'

'Yes, we do have to invite Uncle Lawrence, Lyall,' Carl said. 'He's my brother, in case you hadn't noticed.'

'Yeah,' said Saskia. 'If brothers weren't compulsory, Lyall, I could get out of having you ...' Ouchhh!' she said as Lyall punched her in the arm.

Mum lowered her voice so that only I could hear her. 'I'll deal with you later, Sunny,' she said. 'Just let me get through this wedding first.'

Steph and I went down to Settimio's right after she'd finished feeding Flora and had given the little sleeping bundle over to Mum.

'Try to be sensitive, Sunny,' Mum said. 'It's just a very big misunderstanding.'

Settimio's front door was open and Steph called out, 'Knock knock! It's just me, Settimio.'

'Ah, Stephanie. You are already back? Come inside. Oh, and Sunday too, come in. You forget something?'

He still had the cookbook open and was halfway through writing a shopping list. 'For my speciality,' he said, *Torta di Piccione.*

'Pigeon pie?' I asked.

'Si, they are ready now. Tomorrow...' And he made a cutting action across his throat to show exactly what he had in mind for Finn's pigeons.

'No, Settimio!' I shrieked. 'Those pigeons belong to Finn. They are *not* for making pie.'

'But Finn, he leave them here for me to make ready, for the eating.'

'Settimio,' Steph said patiently. 'There seems to be a small misunderstanding. They're homing pigeons. Sunny and Finn are in the middle of training them to become messenger birds. They're not for eating.'

Settimio looked confused. 'But the children ask me to feed them, and they visit me and I tell them they are not ready, but that soon they will be ready – for the wedding.'

'I thought you meant ready for the wedding, like *love doves*, Settimio. You know how people release them at some celebrations? That's what I thought you meant when you said they'd be ready for the wedding. See?'

'But these are not doves. These are pigeons. Pigeons are for eating. For many generations this recipe has been in my family.'

'No no no!' I wailed. 'You just can't eat Finn's pigeons, Settimio.

'But the *Torta di Piccione*. This is my speciality.'

'No no no, Settimio. You can use chicken, duck, turkey, quail. I don't even care if you use a magpie – anything. But you can't make a pie out of Finn's pigeons. It just won't do. Finn raised them from hatchlings. Understand? They're Finn's babies, Settimio.'

'I understand,' he said disappointedly. 'But still I don't know for why you need these pigeons to be messengers. Why not your friend Finn just use a telephone, uh?'

31.

Finally, it was the night before the wedding. Saskia and I were in her room where she was parading her outfit for possibly the twenty-seventh time.

'And I thought I'd wear these too,' she said, holding up a pair of dangly earrings. 'Or will they clash with my shoes? What do you think, Sunny?

'Oh, that reminds me,' I said. 'I have to go up to the attic and get something.'

'I'll wait here,' Saskia said. 'Who knows what sort of monster wildlife might be lurking up there.'

Carl had left the ladder to the attic down and I climbed towards the darkness, before finding the light switch. I found the box labelled *miscellaneous*. And as I was feeling about for the things I'd hidden inside it I realised that thinking about Granny Carmelene didn't make me feel sad any more, not one little bit. It occurred to me that I hadn't needed Bruce and Terry in weeks, not since I'd made *nowhere* into a kind of *somewhere* (and not the type of somewhere I needed proof of).

'That's exactly what we were thinking, Ms Hathaway.'

Bruce's voice gave me a fright, but not half as much as other frights I'd had lately. Bruce and Terry were sitting on two old chairs that clearly needed re-upholstering.

'Oh, hello, you two,' I said, just as I found Granny Carmelene's locket. 'I thought I could clean this up a bit and wear it to the wedding. Maybe I could even wear one of Granny's dresses too.'

Terry cleared his throat and said, 'Sunny, we need to have a little talk. Don't we, Bruce?'

'Terry's right,' said Bruce, looking uncomfortable. 'It's just that, well, we've been feeling a little under-utilised lately. And well, it's like this …'

Terry stood up, being careful not to bang his head on the low sloping ceiling. 'It's like this, see, Sunny?' he continued. 'We've been offered what you might call *another assignment* and all things considered …'

'Are you sacking me?' I asked. 'What about the Woe-Be-Gone grief repellent?'

'We'll be taking that too,' said Bruce. 'Like I said, we've been offered a new assignment. But it's, ah, confidential.'

I'd never considered being sacked by a figment of my very own imagination, but Bruce and Terry seemed dead serious. 'What about if I need you back again?' I asked, just to make sure I could still have a little control.

But their answer came back all muffled, as if they were talking under water, and I couldn't understand a thing. And at the very same time, Bruce and Terry went all fuzzy, like when there's no aerial in the TV, and soon I could hardly see them. Then they became just an outline before disappearing completely.

'Guys?' I said, just to be sure. 'Hello!'

I switched off the light and went downstairs to polish up Granny Carmelene's locket. Bruce and Terry were right. I really didn't need them any more. And I was even a little relieved that *they* had sacked *me*, because, in case you hadn't noticed, I'm really not very good at saying goodbye.

I was woken the next morning by Flora noises, so I hopped straight out of bed and headed for Steph's room. Flora had a brand-new formal baby-dress especially for the wedding, with tiny little flowers embroidered along the front.

'When can we put it on her?' asked Saskia as Steph was changing Flora's nappy.

'Let's wait until just before the guests arrive,' said Steph, checking her watch. I could tell she was feeling a little nervous because Dad wasn't home from the airport yet and I guess she was worried he'd be late and miss the wedding.

'It's only ten o'clock, Steph,' I said, hoping to make her feel better. 'He'll be here soon. Don't worry.'

I was excited for Dad to get home too, because Steph was seeming more herself than ever, more like the person she was before Flora was born and she somehow forgot who she used to be. (Privately I thought it was probably because of the rose-petal medicine.) Nothing seemed to matter to me quite as much as making sure Steph was feeling okay. It was as if she was at the top of the family food pyramid. Steph had to be okay for Flora to be okay, and Flora had to be okay for me and Dad to be okay, and for everyone else in our little odd-bod world to be okay.

Carl was blasting Nat King Cole music (in Spanish) while the catering people and the linen people and the flower people and the bar people traipsed in and out of the house.

'We couldn't have asked for a more perfect day,' he said, whizzing through the kitchen in his bathrobe. 'Just glorious!'

Saskia bounded in carrying a shoebox full of place cards she'd made for the table. 'Finished!' she said. 'Look, Dad!'

Carl managed to slow down for a millisecond to pick a tag out of the box.

'They look wonderful, darling, but I'm afraid this one

has a slight spelling error. You seem to have your 'p's and 'b's a little mixed up.'

Lyall looked up from his bowl of cereal.

'Gee, Saskia,' he said with his mouth full. 'Isn't that just what *dyslexic* people do?'

Carl pulled a handful of cards out of the box and spread them on the table. Sure enough, practically all of them had mistakes.

'I don't get it,' said Saskia, holding up a card saying *puster conroy*. 'They look perfectly normal to me.'

Just then Mum appeared looking frantic. She had a mud pack all over her face which was at various stages of drying and cracking. I wondered how she could let Carl see her like that. On her wedding day! I mean, what if he changed his mind and unproposed?

Lyall must have been thinking the same thing. 'Hey! I didn't think you guys were meant to see each other until the ceremony,' he said, shovelling down some more cereal. 'Isn't it, like, bad luck or something?'

Mum chuckled (as best she could with her dry-mud skin.) 'Second time around you kind of free-form it a little more. Lyall, did you empty all the bins? And I want you kids to stay out of the caterers' way. They're going to need full reign of the kitchen soon.'

Carl swept the place cards back into the box before Mum could see them.

'They're perfect,' he said to Saskia. 'Thank you for all your hard work.' Then he turned to Mum and gave her a hug and said, 'I'd still marry you even if you did turn up to the wedding like that, darl.'

Mum tried her best to smile, but she couldn't move her face. 'That's very sweet of you, Carl,' she said, keeping her lips as still as possible.

All three of us kids took the hug as a cue to immediately leave the room. Even Willow leapt at the chance to follow me upstairs.

But we'd only made it halfway up when Dad arrived home, causing us all to run straight back down again.

'Hello!' he shouted, trying to contain Willow.

I ran and gave him a big hug. 'You made it!' I said.

'Hi, James!' squeaked Saskia. 'I'll go tell Steph!'

Steph had taken in a beautiful dress of Granny Carmelene's until it fitted me perfectly, and Granny's old locket was gleaming like new. I hoped Granny didn't mind me taking out the photograph of Grandpa Henry, but I really wanted to replace it with one of Flora (and maybe one day I'd even have one of Finn too). I also hoped Granny didn't mind me wearing her dress with my chunky lace-up boots and just the right amount of stripy sock. I mean, when you're wearing a dead person's outfit, sometimes you just have to mix it up a little.

The doorbell didn't stop *ding-donging* all morning. I had just finished doing my hair when Mum called to me from downstairs.

'Sunny, Finn's here!'

'Coming!' I shouted.

Mum and Carl had been a little frantic because Croque Monsieur, their favourite gypsy band who were playing at the wedding, were running late. But just as I reached the landing, the doorbell rang again and thankfully it was them. Mum ushered the band into the library. I was relieved to see that she had washed off her mud pack before answering the door to Finn.

I had my hair all plaited into a Frida Kahlo styles, and I'd even put on a little eye stuff and lip gloss from the make-up kit Claud had bought me for my birthday.

'Wow, Sunny Hathaway,' said Finn. 'Don't you look good? Mad boots.' Finn had a fresh flower in the lapel of and was wearing his pin-striped jacket, and matching suit pants and a tie as well.

'You look really good too, Finn Fletcher-Lomax,' I said. 'What's that stuff in your hair?'

'Brylcreem,' he said, running one hand through his slicked-back hair. 'Just like Elvis Presley.'

'Did you bring the pigeons?'

'Yep. Did you make the box?'

'Saskia did, actually.'

Finn and I had planned for him to bring the three pigeons from his house so that we could release them all after Mum and Carl had said their vows. (Releasing a box of pigeons would also be the perfect distraction if Mum and Carl cringed us all out by doing one of those really long kisses.) Saskia had made a special box and painted it all pearly white and silver.

'I was going to bring some rice too,' said Finn. 'But the birds might just hang about and eat it instead of flying off.'

'Hardly very dramatic,' I said.

'Exactly,' said Finn.

Just before twelve the guests (including Claud's family and Buster) started arriving and Carl asked Lyall to make a sign for the front door saying, *Please Come Around the Back.* Carl was all dressed up but in a smart-casual linen-shirt-and-pants kind of way.

'Now you kids better go out and entertain our guests. Alex and I won't be coming out until the ceremony.'

'And you can all help the bar staff hand around drinks too,' added Carl.

'Jeez, Dad,' said Lyall. 'Is there ever a time we don't have to do jobs?'

Outside everything looked absolutely perfect. There was one huge long table with a long stripy canopy over it in case it rained. There were flowers from the garden running all the way down the centre of the table, and arrangements of fig leaves, ivy and grapes. Even Saskia's funny place cards looked perfect. And when Croque Monsieur started playing their gypsy music, it really did make everything feel like the most jubilant and grand of special occasions

It was a weird feeling, though, being a guest in your own home and standing around the garden just *chatting*. Pretty soon, all us kids were huddled together and Buster had plotted a potential escape plan up the river by boat if things became drastically dull.

'No one would even notice,' said Buster. 'If we wait till after lunch and all. We could just sneak off on *Queenie* while everyone's dancing.'

Claud and I rolled our eyes at one another.

'Ah, I hate to break it to you, Buster,' I said, 'but I'm pretty sure Mum and Carl actually *would* notice if I was suddenly to disappear from their *wedding*.'

'Dad would *definitely* notice,' agreed Saskia. 'We'd be grounded for life.'

'Maybe another day?' said Finn hopefully. 'It's a nice idea.'

Croque Monsieur, who had been weaving their music all around the garden while the guests were arriving, suddenly appeared at the top of the back steps and burst out another gutsy tune. Then they formed a line with the accordionist in front and led the way down the stairs towards the arched gateway to the orchard, which was where the actual wedding part was going to take place. It was fully covered with roses.

And then Mum and Carl appeared at the back door. (I could tell Mum was doing her best to keep a straight face, because she has a tendency to giggle right at the moments you're not meant to.)

I have to say that for a middle-aged person, Mum looked as special as anything. Maybe it was becuase of the mud pack?

'Alex looks *really* pretty,' whispered Saskia, and the whole crowd grew quiet as Mum and Carl made their way to the arch.

Finn had stashed the pigeon box under one of the tablecloths at the bar, so it wouldn't get in anybody's way.

'You better go get it now,' I whispered. 'Imagine if right in the middle of the ceremony, Willow found them and caused a scene.' Finn's eyes grew wide in agreement and he slipped through the crowd towards the bar.

I have to be honest, I was thinking the next part would be dead boring. The actual wedding part, I mean. I was kind of just hanging out for *And now you can kiss the bride*, which of course was our cue for pigeon-releasing and rose petal throwing. But I was wrong about the ceremony being boring. Mum and Carl's celebrant actually cracked the odd joke and all the things he spoke about were really interesting. Lyall and Saskia and I each had small roles. Lyall had to produce the rings and Saskia and I were in charge of everything to do with flowers. Saskia had even put flowers around Willow's collar.

Very quickly it was crunch time, and you could tell Lyall was super-relieved to hand over the rings so that he no longer had to worry about losing them. The photographer was down on one knee hoping to get just the right shot, and other people in the crowd got their cameras ready to snap away at the very moment that Mum and Carl officially transformed from divorcee-defacto crossword freaks to *Husband and Wife*.

Finn and the box of pigeons were in position just as Mum and Carl started kissing and Croque Monsieur burst into another tune over the clapping and cheering.

Saskia and I threw rose-petal confetti high up into the air over Mum and Carl, and Finn opened the lid right at the perfect time. All six birds flapped away, their wings whistling loud enough to make Mum and Carl pause from their kiss and look up. And I tossed some more confetti right at the perfect time for the photographer to capture the whole thing. (I was hoping like crazy that those birds didn't do anything disastrous like poo on Mum and Carl, even though that photo might make a really good one for the bloopers section of the wedding album.)

The whole crowd clapped and cheered as the birds flew out of sight, and Mum and Carl looked as thrilled as can be.

Croque Monsieur broke into one of those songs that you couldn't help clapping along to, and pretty soon the whole crowd were clapping in unison and it seemed like a perfectly natural thing to do to form a circle of clapping around Mum and Carl. Then the music sped up a little and there was no choice other than for the circle to dance around them.

Smaller circles formed in the bigger circle and broken circles joined up again to make new circles as everybody grabbed the hand of whoever was next to them. I tell you, if Croque Monsieur can make weddings so much fun it made me wonder if they shouldn't also be booked for funerals. Maybe if I'd had Croque Monsieur around I wouldn't have needed Bruce and Terry or any Woe-Be-Gone fast-knockdown grief spray.

Mum and Carl were the first to sit down for lunch and the band mellowed out a little while all the guests found their places. When everyone was settled, Mum and Carl stood and thanked everyone for coming. The waiters had made sure everyone had a fresh glass of champagne (except us kids who got fruit punch) and Carl held his glass high and said, 'To our blessed family and friends, Alex and I would like to welcome you and thank you for all your love and support. Now, please make yourselves at home and help us enjoy our wedding feast!'

Then Lyall stood up, held his fruit punch high and said, 'To Alex and Carl'.

At which, the whole wedding party stood and answered in chorus, 'To Alex and Carl,'

It was a feast all right. There was something for everyone (although Settimio did miss out on his pigeon pie).

'Yum, this is like one of those *all you can eat* joints,' said Buster, adding another prawn tail to the pile on his side plate. Claud looked a little embarrassed. Maybe she was finally losing her fascination with bogans.

'But then again,' said Claud, 'you don't *have* to eat all you can eat you know, Buster. It's pretty.... um ...'

'Pretty bogan,' said Saskia, looking Buster straight in the eye as he licked his fingers one by one.

I blurted out the first thing I could think to change the topic. 'Come on, Buster,' I said. 'Let's all do some more dancing.'

'Na, too full. I'd chuck for sure,' he said, leaning back on his chair and undoing the top button on his pants.

'Eeew!' Saskia squeaked. and then, 'Eeew grooossss!' as Buster let out a huge gassy burp.

'Let's dance then,' suggested Finn, trying to take the focus away from Buster's bodily functions.

'Yes, let's dance!' said Saskia. 'Dad and Alex are dancing again too!'

'Come on, Lyall,' I said, tugging his jacket sleeve. 'Look, Ritchie and Kara are even up!'

After a while even Buster and Claud joined in, and I took some time out to grab Carl's camera and get some good footage of the dance floor. It was then that my eye was caught by something down the other end of the table.

I zoomed in and focused the camera on Steph

For a moment I thought she was crying, but on closer inspection I realised she was actually heaving with laughter.

'What do you think Steph's finding so hilarious?' I said to Finn.

She and Settimio were deep in some sort of a conversation. The sort of conversation that made them lean in toward one another, like they were swapping secrets in class, then both pull back and roar with laughter.

'Let's go find out,' I said to Finn. 'I've hardly spoken to Steph all day.'

'Oh, Sunny,' said Steph as we walked up, wiping a tear from her eye and trying to compose herself. 'I haven't laughed so much in years.'

Finn and I shared Dad's empty chair and waited patiently for Steph to fill us in on the joke.

Lyall plonked himself down on one of the empty seats opposite Settimio and Steph. Saskia was close behind.

Settimio was still giggling and looking very red in the

face, and I noticed Dad making his way over with Flora, who had finally fallen asleep.

'Can you tell the story again, Settimio?' said Steph. 'That's if you're comfortable to, of course.'

'What's going on?' asked Buster.

'Gosh,' said Steph. 'Suddenly we have a whole audience.'

'I was just telling Stephanie how I brok-ed my leg.'

Steph burst out laughing again. 'I'm sorry, Settimio,' she choked.

'Tell us!' we begged. 'Pleeease!'

'Okay, I will tell. But you have to promise not to laugh.'

'We promise!' I said, wondering why he was asking us not to laugh when he and Steph looked as if they were possibly about to *die* laughing.

Settimio took a deep breath and looked me straight in the eye.

'Okay... It was just after your grandmother die and I am in my cottage and I am alone. Very sad time. So I am lying in bed and it is the middle of night and I wake to go to the bathroom. It is very dark, but I don't turn on light because I am very sleepy. So I walk very slowly looking for door. Like this.' Settimio held his arms out in front of him the way people do when they are pretending to be Frankenstein or a zombie.

'So, I am walking in this manner, trying to find door,

but I walk straight into edge of door headfirst. *Bang!* It hit me right here on my nose!'

'Ow, so that's why you had a cut on your nose!'

'*Si*, and I am thinking maybe I brok-ed the nose as well.'

'Ow,' we all said at once. Steph was trying her hardest not to laugh again.

'Okay, so my head, it is very sore; and my nose, there is blood. So I go to the bathroom where I have medicine cabinet. This time, I turn on light and see there is lot of blood! So first I take toilet paper and I use for the nose. I go through lot of paper in this manner, so I throw in toilet and I repeat with some more until there is not so much blood. Then I take from cabinet the cotton wool and I have some – I forget how you say, like some alcohol for making clean the wounds.'

'Disinfectant?' Saskia says.

'Yes, like this sort of thing, but like spirit alcohol. Old-fashioned thing. So I put much of this on cotton wool and I hold on nose for long time, in this manner.' Settimio pinched the bridge of his nose with one hand to demonstrate.

'So, after much time like this I am still bleeding. I throw old cotton wool into toilet and get new one with more alcohol. I am very tired so I think I will sit down. And because I am in bathroom I think best place to sit down is on toilet.'

'Totally,' said Lyall. 'I would have done that.'

'So, I sit for a long time, maybe five, maybe ten minutes, holding nose, and I think to myself, *maybe bleeding has stopped*? So I check and I see that it has so I throw cotton wool into toilet. Then I think, *Aaah, it is all over. Now, I have a cigarette.*'

'Ew. I didn't know you smoked!' I said.

'This was the *last* time I smok-ed a cigarette, actually,' said Settimio.

'So *then* what happened?' asked Saskia.

'Well, I take cigarette; I sit back down on toilet; I light cigarette with match; I throw match in toilet and… *BANG!*'

'Oh my god!' gasped Lyall. 'An explosion!'

'Yes! Because there is so much paper in the toilet from the brok-ed nose and the paper is soaked in spirit alcohol, it goes *BANG* and there is a whoosh of flame and I burn-ed my behind!'

We all broke into hysterical laughter, even Settimio.

'So now, I have brok-ed the nose, I have burn-ed the behind and I fall on the floor. I think to myself that I now need to see doctor, but I can not drive and there is no one here so I crawl to the phone and I call for ambulance and they are coming to get me, so I wait for them, still on floor.'

'Poor you,' I say, wishing I'd never had a mean thought

277

about Settimio. No wonder he'd been so grumpy.

'That's not all,' said Steph, laughing again.

'Then what, Settimio?'

'So, I am waiting on floor and ambulance come and they look how I have burn-ed the behind and how I have brok-ed the nose, and they say I have to go with them to hospital for overnight. They put me on stretcher and I have to lie on my side because of my behind. So, two men, they pick me up and have to carry me on stretcher to ambulance.'

'That's quite a long way,' I said.

'Yes, it is far. And on the way they are talking to me and they are asking me about how I injure myself in such a manner.'

Steph burst out laughing again and Settimio was laughing so much he could hardly speak.

'So … I tell them about door and nose and about how cigarette mak-ed the fire while I am sitting on the toilet. And when I tell them how I fall on the floor … they laugh so much … one of them … he *drop* stretcher … and I fall off onto ground … and I *brok-ed the leg*!'

We were all laughing so much we could hardly breathe, and I was even worried that Settimio might fall off his chair and cause another injury.

And seeing Steph laughing like that (or as Settimio would say, *in this manner)* took me back to that wintry day in the rose garden when Saskia and I collected petals to make Steph's flower-essence remedy. And how I'd dreamt myself a daydream where Steph was laughing, even though no one had seen her laugh in months, especially not her own sad self. And in the end, that one little daydream had closed its eyes on itself until it woke again to the music of Mum and Carl's favourite gypsy band, to become a brand new moment.

Settimio wiped his eyes and took Steph and me by the hand, coaxing us up off our chairs.

'We have laughed; we have cried,' he said. 'Now it is time to dance.'

I did remember to include my flowchart!
See page 100 if you've forgotten about it.

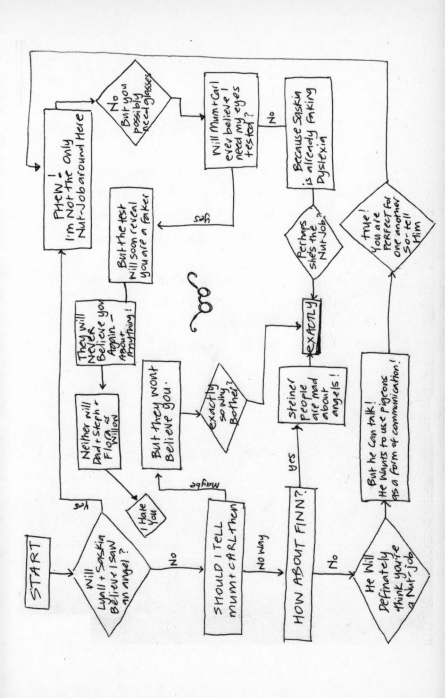

About the author

Marion Roberts always wanted to be a fashion designer, but she studied science, alternative medicine and psychotherapy instead. She also worked as a chef and taught people how to cook. Marion started writing because she wanted a job she could do in her pyjamas. Also, her friends kept saying her emails were too long, and she needed to find another place to put her stories. She was born in Melbourne, which has always been her hometown. Her first book, *Sunny Side Up*, was published in 2008.

Acknowledgements

Thanks to Oscar, John, Lucian and Ava for being the blessed people I call home. Thanks to my lovely friends (bad influence ones included). Thanks to everyone at Allen & Unwin for supporting and encouraging me through the writing of this book, in particular Jodie Webster and Susannah Chambers. Thanks to Sophie Hynes for her fabulous drawing. Thanks to my cat, Arthur, who slept and purred on my arm through every draft, and to Willow, for the very fond role she plays in my memory.

Start with one quiet, perfect life.

add: 1 step-dad
2 precooked siblings
1 best friend
1 sworn enemy
and a long-lost grandmother

Flavour with a dash of secrets,
a pinch of jealousy and a good
dollop of growing-up.

Cook on high all summer long.

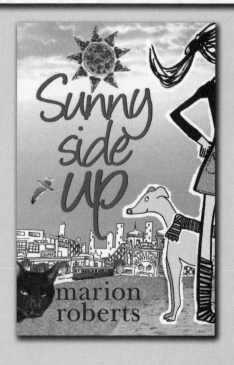

Spend more time with Sunny Hathaway.
Her first adventure will knock your socks off!

Wings To Fly

PATRICK COOPER

PATRICK COOPER

Wings
TO Fly

Andersen Press • London

First published in 2001 by
Andersen Press Limited,
20 Vauxhall Bridge Road, London SW1V 2SA
www.andersenpress.co.uk

British Library Cataloguing in Publication Data available
ISBN 1 84270 026 X

*Photograph of biplane on back cover reproduced with the permission of the
Trustees of the Imperial War Museum, London.*

Typeset by FiSH Books, London WC1
Printed and bound in Great Britain by the Guernsey Press Company Ltd.,
Guernsey, Channel Islands